Phantom Rage

The Rage Trilogy: Book 1

by

William Blackwell

Cover Designed by Telemachus Press, LLC
    Published by Telemachus Press, LLC at Smashwords
    ISBN: 978-1-0697318-0-7 (paperback)
    Version: 2017.01.01

Acknowledgements

Heartfelt thanks to my loyal and supportive readers, friends and family, the hardworking staff at Telemachus Press, Winslow Eliot and paranormal investigators Brad Dotten and Tom Davis. Special thanks to the Government of Prince Edward Island for its financial support.

To my dear friends Brian and Brenda, for helping me become a better person.

Darkness cannot drive out darkness: only light can do that.
–Martin Luther King Jr.

Phantom Rage

The Rage Trilogy: Book 1

CHAPTER ONE

I'm going to die. They're going to kill me. My boyfriend's going to dump me. My health is failing. I can't breathe. I'm going crazy. I'm going to get fired. My life is over. I can't pay my bills. I'm fucked!

Kathleen Freeborne felt the pain in her left hand first as she lay in bed and a barrage of negative thoughts overwhelmed her mind. Then she felt the tingling, stinging sensation creep up her arm, penetrate her shoulder, slice through her neck, finally finding an unwelcome home in the left side of her head. It began throbbing dully, growing in intensity, starting off as a thumbtack-sized ache, slowly enveloping her entire brain.

She winced and her eyes narrowed. Her palms were sweaty. Beads of perspiration rolled down her forehead, into her eyes. One landed on her upper lip and she absently rolled her tongue over it, the salty taste reminding her of reality.

Deep breaths. You're being paranoid.

She inhaled deeply and exhaled slowly, but the crippling thoughts continued.

You're fucked. You can't manage your life. Shit is about to hit the fan. In a big way. You don't have your act together. At all. And Mark knows it. He's going to leave you.

She didn't dare move, worried that to get up would be problematic. Her hands instinctively clutched the thick comforter that by now had slipped down, only covering her lower torso. Her knuckles turned white with the force of her

7

grip as a wave of panic swept through her body and she shuddered.

Thirty minutes later the wave of despair subsided, her mind went completely blank momentarily and then cleared. She slowly released her tight grip on the comforter and looked out the bedroom window, streams of sunlight shining through the Venetian blinds painting white lines across her slender frame. She blinked, wiped her eyes with sweat-soaked hands and slowly her thoughts returned to normal. The pain subsided.

And she remembered. Her life wasn't bad. Actually, it was very good. At 32, she had managed to focus her efforts successfully. Living in a rented two-bedroom apartment in the town of Montague, Prince Edward Island, she had settled into a comfortable relationship with Mark Riley, and they had been together for four years. Sure, the relationship had its ups and downs. Don't they all? But, overall, she was very happy with Mark. He understood her and not everyone understood the complexity of Kathleen Freeborne's mind and the analytical way in which she processed information.

Intellectually, Mark was probably inferior to Kathleen but that didn't bother her. He had a street-smarts about him that fascinated and attracted her. And, she wasn't sure she wanted an intellectual equal. Maybe they didn't have a lot in common, but that didn't bother her either.

On the contrary, she thought their personalities complimented each other. She tended to worry and Mark had a calmness and inner peace about him that she found reassuring.

Looking in the mirror at her sweaty image, the little crease in her brow, long brown hair, clear brown eyes, she frowned as she noticed the corners of her lips pointing downward. They usually pointed up and her friends often commented her smile was infectious and could light up a room. She forced a smile, trying to recreate the attractive features that many had told her she possessed.

The smile came and went, the corners of her lips returning to their downward position. It was not her usual smile. She furrowed her brow, ran her hands through her thick mane, sighed, peeled off her sweaty white undershirt and panties and got in the shower.

The hot water cascading off her fit body made her feel a little better. But she had to admit the fear and panic she had felt immediately after waking up this morning had scared the hell out of her.

In her entire life she had never suffered from an anxiety attack.

She remembered the condition in others from her college days, five years ago. She had completed a three-year diploma program in human services and the last year she had specialized in autism and behavioral sciences. Afterward, she found a job with the local school board as an educational assistant, teaching autistic children aged 9 to 11 years.

It paid well and she enjoyed the challenge. But she wondered now, as she stepped out of the bathroom, toweling herself dry, if it was the stressful situations at work that had triggered the anxiety attack. On a few occasions she had been punched in the face by her students. In another incident, one enraged student had locked both hands onto her hair, and it had taken two staff tugging furiously to finally remove him.

Or maybe it was the latest incident with the control freak teacher, Ron Bagland. There had been an incident with one of the students acting up while Ron was absent and the principal had agreed to call in Child Welfare Services, after consulting with the educational assistants.

When Ron heard about the incident a few days later, he had entered the small classroom, yelling and screaming at the three educational assistants, right in front of the six autistic students.

Kathleen's friend and colleague Linda Wellington had broken down in tears during the outburst. Kathleen remembered the tears welling up in her eyes and how she too had struggled to maintain her composure. A few days later Linda had mentioned she was looking for another job.

Are teachers supposed to yell at their assistants in this day and age? Right in front of the students? I don't think so.

Kathleen made a mental note to call her physician as she dressed and walked over to her wall calendar, reminding herself of the date: Saturday, February 25th, 2012. She looked at the clock: 11:56 am. She picked up her landline and dialed Dr. Frank Heeling, wondering grimly what would happen if she ever had an anxiety attack at work. She shuddered as the phone rang, trying to force the thought from her mind.

CHAPTER TWO

10:56 pm, two nights earlier, King's Playhouse Theatre, Georgetown, Prince Edward Island, Atlantic coast, Canada.

It has become public knowledge among many residents of this small, laid-back island province that this theatre, erected in 1897 on former burial grounds, is haunted. There are reports of doors opening and closing, lights mysteriously turning on and off, items disappearing, strange voices and even actual ghost sightings.

One of Canada's longest running theatres, it carries on business as usual and is a major cultural and entertainment venue in PEI.

Caretaker Bill Blythe wasn't concerned about culture and entertainment as he finished up mopping the hallways, nearing the end of his shift. In his mid-sixties, he was happy to be there on this frigid and stormy night. It kept him away from his cantankerous wife, Thelma, who was always reminding him of what he had forgotten to do.

"You forgot to take the garbage out ... you forgot to clean the hair from the soap after you showered ... you forgot to shovel the snow ... you forgot to put the dishes in the dishwasher ... if you're going to the kitchen anyway, why don't you take your plate with you?"

It was always something with her. She had become miserable in her old age and Bill thought the longer he was with her the more her negativity rubbed off on him. He had been with her for twenty-five years, but it seemed to him things had turned particularly ugly within the last two years.

Leaving for work a few hours earlier she had been quick to remind him to shovel the snow "either before you go or before you set foot back in this house."

"Yes dear," was all he had managed for a reply.

It seemed all Thelma did now was watch television, eat junk food and complain.

Usually a happy-go-lucky sort, his demeanor had slowly begun to change. He had become much less patient with people, more agitated and had started indulging in alcohol more than he cared to admit. The King's Playhouse was an escape for him, a place to get away from Thelma's nagging and find solace in the numbing effects of the booze and the solitude of the empty building.

What a way to retire, he thought, as he set his mop down, reached into the pocket of his worn blue coveralls and took a nip from the flask. The strong taste of Lamb's Navy Rum burned his mouth and his esophagus on its way down, but he smiled, a crooked, toothy grin and brushed his grey, grizzled beard with his hand. The liquid warmed his insides and numbed his feelings, which is what he wanted right now.

"How you doing Captain?" he asked, waving a hand to an empty chair the Town Council had set aside for the ghost of the theatre, whom it had named Captain George. The Town figured if there was a ghost, it would accommodate him so he could enjoy the shows along with the patrons.

The empty chair did not respond to Bill's question. He paused, waiting for an answer but one was not forthcoming.

Retired with a pension, he had taken the caretaker position at the theatre four years ago to keep himself occupied, give him something to do to take his mind of what had become a mundane existence. Now, dealing with you-know-who, the job had become something he looked forward to. It was fast becoming the only thing he looked forward to.

He had gotten used to the eerie sounds of the theatre. Lights often turned on and off, at times he heard footsteps, even the odd door slamming. But he had never heard any voices, or screams, or seen any actual ghosts.

But he hoped that one day he would. He had become lonely and wanted someone to talk to. Even if it were a ghost.

"Anything on your mind, Captain?" he asked the empty chair in the dimly lit hallway as he took another long pull on the flask. He waited for a response, but all he heard was the high-pitched whistling of the wind outside. He knew it was snowing hard—the weatherman had predicted 15 centimetres—but he was in staggering distance to his house so he didn't care.

And tonight he wanted to get a little more than buzzed—he wanted to get shit-faced.

He finished his last mop-stroke, put it inside the bucket on wheels, and pushed it into the utility room. He emptied the dirty water into the sink, rinsed the mop and leaned it into a corner alongside the bucket. He reached into his pocket for the flask, stopped and listened.

He heard a low shrieking sound, coming from the stage area. He returned the flask to his pocket, without taking a swig and listened again. All he could hear was the wind whistling, the odd creak of the old building, probably from its powerful force. Nothing that would concern him in any way.

He opened the flask and took a long pull. He wanted to see something. "Come out, come out, wherever you are," he said, closing the door to the utility room and entering the theatre. He pulled out his flashlight and walked toward the stage. He didn't want to turn any lights on. If it were a ghost, he didn't want to scare it.

He sat down on the stage and pointed the flashlight beam at the ceiling, enjoying the flashing light patterns he was creating. "Come out and play with me."

Silence.

Suddenly the round flashlight beam on the ceiling grew a pair of eyes, a sinister smile. He blinked, wiped his eyes, returned his gaze to the beam. The eyes remained. The smile remained. Then something strange happened—something that would haunt Bill Blythe for the rest of his life.

A white apparition grew from the beam of light, floated down and stood in front of him. It transformed into a small man dressed as a priest, small horned-rimmed spectacles, neatly-cropped grey hair, signature white collar.

The beady eyes regarded Bill. "You need to be saved," Reverend James Maling said, smiling.

Bill, by this time, had a little alcoholic glow on. But he couldn't help shivering as the room became cold. He could feel the hairs on his neck stand up—took another swig of liquid confidence to settle his nerves and asked, "Saved from what?"

"Saved from whom," Maling said.

There was a moment's pause as Bill digested the sentence. "Okay. I'll play along. Saved from whom?"

"Your wife Thelma. You need to be saved from her. Do you want that?"

"Why the heck not," Bill said without hesitation.

In a swift motion, the apparition of Maling possessed the body of Bill Blythe. He shuddered as it became one with his worn out body. Noticing his core temperature dropping, he reached for the flask.

His mind went blank as Reverend James Maling flung it away. It hit the wall with a tinny popping sound and the rum sprayed out, staining it a yellowish brown, the image of a smiling serpent barely detectable.

Maling prided himself on being a well-respected man of the cloth. He had a certain disdain for self-indulgence and he was not prepared to conduct his important business intoxicated.

CHAPTER THREE

Mark Riley drove south along the Highway 4 in his black 1993 Chevy Silverado ¾ ton diesel pick-up truck on a sunny but cold Saturday afternoon. In his mind it was a truck with a mission of its own and he had affectionately named it Black Death.

Sure Black Death would creak and groan at times, but the old war horse always managed to get the job done, regardless of how difficult it might be. Mark believed they shared something in common.

At 33, his lower back gave him constant pain in spite of all the medication he had to take—five different prescriptions. Sometimes he felt like an old war horse as well.

At least the pills reduce the pain to a dull roar, he thought, as he fiddled with the stereo, trying to pick up a station. Finally he found the Eagles, singing *Take It Easy*, and adjusted his seating position, wincing slightly until he found the spot of least resistance.

He had had the misfortune to be rear-ended two years ago while hauling debris from a Charlottetown residence that had been destroyed by nasty tenants. The injury had left him with three herniated disks in his back. One surgery later, a half a dozen different chiropractors, and he still felt in almost as much pain as he did on that fateful day his 1992 Toyota Corolla had careened out into oncoming traffic—the result of the collision—zigzagged uncontrollably and finally smashed into a power pole. He had been completely paralyzed for a month after the accident before he was finally able to walk.

Normally the thought would bring a slight frown to his boyish good looks, but today it made him smile. He had found out yesterday afternoon his lawyer had finally reached a settlement with the female driver's insurance company. He was only a week away from getting his hands on a check for $80,000, the largest lump-sum of cash he would probably ever come across in his life.

He knew it wouldn't be long before he would no longer be able to earn his living hauling garbage and doing odd carpentry contracting jobs. One day soon doctors would tell him he would have to retrain for a desk job.

So the news had made his day. But what had made him even happier was what he planned on doing with the money.

He wanted to buy a house with Kathleen and move in with her. And, so far, he hadn't told her of the settlement—he planned on surprising her tonight on their way to the paranormal investigation of the King's Playhouse Theatre.

Mark had always been fascinated with the paranormal and a few years ago a few of his friends—and his girlfriend—had formed PEIPI, Prince Edward Island Paranormal Investigators. The non-profit organization had so far performed twenty investigations.

Unlike Hollywood movies, most of the team's investigations didn't produce any conclusive paranormal activity. Most of it could be explained scientifically. Usually, when they did find something, it was a week or so later during an analysis of the data that a strange voice or image would catch their attention.

And, in some cases, the clients who had supposedly witnessed hauntings wanted some kind of validation they weren't crazy. The team wasn't always able to give them that validation.

Other times, significant stress or a myriad of different drugs would produce strange and interesting images or occurrences the team could not validate as paranormal.

However, on a very few occasions they had seen and photographed orbs, experienced extreme temperature drops and rapidly draining flashlight batteries, heard footsteps, doors slamming, voices, and in one case screams. Kathleen had even been poked by an apparition and on one investigation some of their gear had mysteriously disappeared.

Through research and subsequent advice, PEIPI had even helped a handful of clients live with their ghosts, if not their demons.

Marks phone rang just as he pulled in front of the tenant-occupied property he had been hired to remove debris from. He pulled onto the shoulder of Iona Road and smiled as he recognized his girlfriend's phone number.

"Hi, honey," he said. "How are you?"

"Mark, are you busy?"

"I'm just about to start a job. I have a few minutes."

"I had an anxiety attack this morning and it scared me. I have an appointment next week with my doctor to find out what's wrong. I feel a little stressed. Worried. I don't know if I should come tonight."

"Anxiety attack? You've never had anything like that before, have you?"

"No."

Mark frowned as he digested the information. "It's your call, babe. If you don't feel up to it, don't go."

"I don't know. Can we talk about it later, when you're done?"

Mark looked at his watch: 1:36 pm. "Sure, I'll come over after I dump the first load, maybe two hours."

"Okay. I'd really like to see you. I could use some company."

Mark clicked the phone dead, frowning. *Shit. I thought everything was going so well and now this. What next?*

He rolled in front of the driveway and eyed the chicken-wire fence that had been jury-rigged to block entry. The owner had given him a heads-up earlier, telling him the resident was a psychotic middle-aged female tenant from hell who had been occupying the property for almost a year without paying rent. He had finally managed to get an order of possession that was about to be enforced by the bailiff. It was only a matter of days. In the meantime, his lawyer had told him he had legal possession of the property as the tenant had disregarded a court-ordered eviction notice. The eviction date had come and gone and the woman had ignored it completely.

Mark had been only slightly nervous about accepting the job after he had been told that Joleen De-Yodeler was psychotic. He had become a little more nervous when the owner had given him a phone number of a local RCMP detective, telling him the detective also had his phone number and if there was any trouble at all not to confront the woman but to leave immediately.

He slowly backed up to the chicken-wire fence, remembering the owner had also said the RCMP were stationed nearby. *Why did I take this job, anyway? Oh, right. I felt sorry for the landlord. And I know that bitch Joleen. She's nothing but trouble. She's a waste of space. He told me her history. She's fucked a lot of people over. She needs to pay.*

"Okay, Black Death," he said to his truck, tapping the red dashboard "Let's fix this bitch."

He loved Black Death and often talked to him. He had created a myth around the truck, convincing himself it was much more than a chunk of metal—it was a possessed vehicle capable of deadly force if provoked. *Was it a myth? Or was it Black Death?* Black Death had behaved in mysterious ways in the past so he couldn't be sure.

He stepped on the brake, locked up the four-wheel drive, revved the engine and released the brake. Four tires spun gravel and dirt before finding traction and crunching over the small barricade. He guided the vehicle back rapidly, skidded to a stop in front of the weathered old barn. The property was strewn with debris, geese and ducks.

He stepped out of Black Death. His head still felt a little foggy from his daily medication regiment and he inhaled deeply, trying to clear the cobwebs.

He glanced around quickly, reaching into his pocket for the pepper spray. He had heard there could be a dog or two around. He didn't see any dogs, just ducks and geese squawking and scattering. And garbage. Lots of it. The plastic container calmed his nerves as his fingers gripped the pepper spray trigger momentarily, before bending down to pick up an old chair and toss it into the back of the truck.

This chick is a pack-rat. Or, what do they call them now? Hoarders. She's a hoarder. Don't we have psychologists that specialize in hoarding disorders now?

Mark tossed a few more items in Black Death and suddenly heard a door slam. A heavy-set woman stepped out of the old two-story home and marched purposefully toward him. She had scraggy greyish brown hair, beady grey eyes and a self-righteous attitude.

He could just tell.

Mark had been told she was 55, but she looked a lot older. One thing for sure: she was not aging gracefully. As she neared, he realized there was something in her hand, flashing occasionally as it caught the sun's reflection.

Shit, that's a butcher knife. I better be careful.

"Get off my property," Joleen demanded, waving the knife angrily, coming closer.

Mark ran around to the side of Black Death, pulled out the pepper spray. "I have permission from Nigel, the owner. I have paperwork in the truck that says you're here illegally."

She stopped at the other side of the truck, resting the knife on the box. Her demeanor changed instantly and she smiled, exposing rotten teeth. "Oh Nigel ... we've talked and everything has been straightened out. You don't need to be here now."

Mark knew he only had a few more minutes before he would speed-dial Detective Blaine Redmond of the Montague RCMP detachment. *Ah, what the hell. May as well give her a little more grief. Nigel will be happy. Imagine how much grief she's put him through. He did sound drunk when we talked.*

"I've been hired to do a job," he said. "I've got a wife and kids to support and I won't leave here until I've got a full load."

She pursed her lips in an odd expression. "You're not leaving with my stuff. Unless you want this." She raised the knife, pointed it at him and grinned. "Do you want this?"

Mark fumbled with the pepper spray and then put it back in his pocket. *She's threatening me with a weapon. She can be charged for that.*

He fished out his phone, speed-dialing the cop. Exactly thirty seconds later the Mexican stand-off ended as two cop cars raced up the driveway, sirens blaring, screeching to a halt behind Black Death.

Unfortunately, Joleen saw them coming and retreated into the house with the weapon.

"She threatened me with a butcher knife," Mark told Detective Redmond as he approached.

Redmond, a fit cop in his late thirties with short red hair, had a hard time containing a smile as he walked toward Black Death. *Your time is coming, bitch*, he thought, enjoying the sight of Joleen's face redden with rage.

CHAPTER FOUR

"What if I freak out?"

"As I said honey, it's your call. If you don't feel right, don't come," Mark said, looking concernedly across the kitchen table at Kathleen. They both had large mugs of hot tea in front of them and sipped occasionally as they talked.

After the butcher knife threat, Mark had gone down to the police station to fill out a report. Detective Redmond had an axe to grind with Joleen and wanted Mark to press charges for threatening him. The cop had told him he had pulled her over one day in PEI for a broken taillight and discovered she had no insurance on her vehicle and did not have a driver's license with her.

When she discovered that her shit-box pick-up was going to be towed, she flew into a rage, finally resulting in a police brutality complaint being filed. The police captain had to do something, in spite of the woman's sordid history with the detachment, so Redmond had been demoted to desk duty, pushing pencils for the last six months.

He had vowed to exact his pound of flesh—all within the confines of the law of course.

Initially Mark wasn't sure if he would go through with pressing charges, but after he had called Nigel on his way to see Kathleen, he was leaning toward causing De-Yodeler (he preferred the term Die-Yodeler really, thinking it had a much nicer ring to it and enjoying the sound as it rolled off his tongue) as much grief as possible. She had a history of not only ripping off landlords, but also burning most others she had encountered. If you looked up loser in the dictionary, Mark was sure you would see her ugly mug beside it. She had a complete hatred and disrespect for authority.

Nigel had used a few descriptive profane words as he referred to Die-Yodeler and Mark could tell from the tone of his voice he was happy to cause her some grief. He may have orchestrated the entire clean-up job to do exactly that. Mark could almost feel Nigel smiling on the other end of the long distance call from Vancouver when he had explained to him that Die-Yodeler had freaked out at the sight of Redmond, demanding everyone to get off "her" property. Apparently, the way the tenant laws worked in PEI, even though Nigel had legal possession of his property, the police were not allowed to physically remove her unless they were accompanied by a bailiff. It was insane that a tenant in PEI could remain on a property for free and destroy it for over a year before the paperwork would finally start flowing in the landlord's favor. Apparently, Mark had heard, there was some bleeding heart government regulatory council that basically allowed delinquent tenants to exhaust the appeals process for months—in some cases even years—before justice was finally served.

He had told the story to Kathleen as soon as he had arrived, leaving out some of Nigel's animated profanity, and their discussion had turned to tonight's paranormal investigation.

"But I really want to go," Kathleen said, breaking the pensive silence between them. "I've been looking forward to it for months." She was waiting for some kind of encouragement from Mark, but she could also tell from his concerned expression that he was not prepared to risk something that could potentially put her in harm's way. She knew the decision would have to be hers—and hers alone.

"Honey, only you know if you feel up to it. I can't tell you that."

She had expected the reply. She paused, putting her hands to the hot mug in front of her, the warmth of the tea feeling pleasant on her palms. She couldn't explain it to anyone if she wanted to, but she suddenly felt she had no choice: she had to go.

"That's it, I'm coming," she said.

"Are you sure?" Mark still looked a little worried. "Because, if you're not, we can handle it on our own, you know."

"I'm coming," she said with conviction.

"Okay."

CHAPTER FIVE

At 9:56 pm that night, Black Death rolled along the highway from Montague to Georgetown. The night was clear, the temperature was a few degrees below freezing, and Kathleen noticed with some trepidation the glowing moon was full as she sat alongside Mark.

Jacob McCreery and Angela Dodson, friends and long-time PEIPI investigators, sat in the back seat chatting amicably and flirting.

Nick Calibri, the fifth member of the team couldn't make it and Kathleen was glad for it. His nickname was Mister N, but the N didn't stand for Nick. It meant Mister Negativity. Mister N just processed information in a weird way, putting a negative slant on everything. At one investigation he was convinced a luminescent orb the group had noticed in one of the photos was the presence of a demon, sent from hell to possess and destroy PEIPI. On yet another outing, he had heard the creaking of a door and become hostile, accusing the group of trying to harm him, finally leaving the house and spending the remainder of the night sulking in Black Death. He was prone to panic and paranoia.

Thinking about his personality, Kathleen also realized he had suffered from anxiety attacks for as long as she could remember. But he insisted there was nothing wrong with him and had never bothered to seek help.

She shuddered to think that she and Mister N had anything in common. The group had had a few discussions and planned on removing him from PEIPI, they just had yet to think of a way to do it diplomatically; after all, in spite of his idiosyncrasies, they still considered him a friend.

A friend, at least in Kathleen's case, she could only handle in very small doses. She found if she spent too much time listening to his negativity it started to rub off on her, and she would become mildly depressed. She was feeling out of sorts as it was and didn't want Mister N around to make matters worse.

Prior to leaving, PEIPI had checked to make sure all their equipment was in working order. Kathleen liked to think they took a scientific approach to the paranormal, refusing to bring along an Ouija board or invite psychics or mediums to investigations.

They brought along four walkie-talkies, four high-tech audio-video cameras, two still life digital cameras (which had been altered to see the ultraviolet and infrared spectrum), two digital audio recorders, six LED flashlights, spare batteries (ghosts tend to drain batteries), a few compasses and four new toys they had just acquired from an Australian distributor. The new device, called Mel-8704 Pro Nav Electronic Radiation Tester, performed the dual function of checking room temperature and Electro Magnetic Fields simultaneously.

They also brought motion detectors, notepads and pens. Kathleen liked to write down her emotions, moods and random thoughts as they investigated, making it easier for her to remember them later when the team de-briefed, analyzed and discussed the data.

They used the audio recording equipment in conjunction with various software programs to detect what paranormal investigators refer to as EVPs, or Electronic Voice

Phenomenon; voices undetectable to the human ear but detectable by the audio recorders.

After receiving the green light from King's Playhouse management and Georgetown Town Council—two months in the works—their plan was to spend most of the night at the theatre. They had been told caretaker Bill Blythe would be with them for perhaps an hour or so while they set up their equipment, and then he was supposed to depart, leaving them with a key to lock the building when they were done.

As they pulled into the theatre parking lot on Kent Street, they noticed him sitting on the front steps, smiling at Black Death, seemingly oblivious to the chill.

That's odd, Kathleen thought immediately. The island population was just over 140,000 and, it seemed, everybody knew everybody. Kathleen had known Bill for four years and liked his easy-going and friendly nature. She had often bumped into him shopping at Sobeys supermarket in Montague. His favorite topic of conversation was the weather and he hated the cold. *What's he doing sitting outside if he hates the cold?*

She also noticed his expression was different somehow, more confident and calculating. She couldn't yet put a finger on it.

"You go talk to him," Mark said to her after he parked and began unloading the gear with Jacob and Angela.

"Yeah, he likes you," Angela said with a smile, adjusting her brown baseball cap and winking.

"Did I miss something here?" Jacob asked, reaching into the extended cab for a large duffle bag.

"No, you didn't," Kathleen said, walking toward Bill, who had now stood from his perch on the front steps.

"Nice to see you," he said, extending a hand.

His eyes look different. And he's clean shaven. What's with that?

"You too, Bill," she said, shaking a cold bare hand. "Awfully cold out tonight, eh?"

"Yeah, guess it is."

That's not what he would say. He would say, "It's damn cold and I hate the cold."

"Is the door open Bill?" Mark asked, as the team walked by carrying equipment.

"It is," Bill said.

Kathleen lingered outside, eyeing him curiously as the other investigators went inside.

"You're not going to be here for that long are you?" he asked.

"I thought we had made an arrangement to be here for most of the night?"

"Oh, okay," he said, scratching his chin, which had become red from the cold. "But if you don't find anything?"

"That's a group decision," Kathleen said, mild annoyance creasing her forehead. "We have approval to stay all night if necessary."

"Very well then," Bill said, following her as she walked inside the theatre.

Very well then? Bill doesn't talk like that.

About twenty minutes later, they had most of their equipment set up. Mark and Kathleen were in the basement, Jacob and Angela upstairs in the stage area. They planned on doing two-hour shifts and then rotating.

While they were setting up, Bill had followed Kathleen and Mark closely, asking questions about the equipment, ghosts, religion and on and on. It seemed like he was trying to distract them from their work and had even mentioned a door on the main floor that was now locked and strictly off-limits. Kathleen didn't remember the room to be off-limits when they had been granted permission earlier but it seemed as though Bill was changing the rules as they went.

She was getting annoyed with him and couldn't wait for him to leave.

They sat in the dark in a small room in the basement, one that had apparently been the location of a ghost sighting a few years back. Small flashlights were their only source of light, dimly illuminating small corners of the room. Bill lingered at the doorway, watching them.

Kathleen clicked on her Mel-8704, placed it on the floor a few feet in front of her, and turned on the audio-video recording equipment. She decided there was no time like the present to get rid of him. He was beginning to give her the creeps. And she was starting to feel a sense of fear she had never before encountered during an investigation. Something nagged at the back of her mind and she didn't know if was a precursor to another anxiety attack or something far more dangerous.

And Bill Blythe, if that's who was standing in front of her, wasn't helping matters by loitering.

"You know, I don't believe in ghosts at all," Bill said. "And I'm sure mainstream science doesn't recognize, what did you call it, paranormal?"

Mark rolled his eyes.

"I'm sorry Bill," Kathleen said. "But if you don't mind, we need to conduct our investigation on our own, in silence right now. I'm not trying to be rude, but we were told you would be leaving after we got set up."

Bill looked annoyed, but abruptly his mouth dropped open and his eyes widened. And Kathleen thought she saw something contort his weathered features that she hadn't noticed before. And that something was dread.

What's he hiding?

She glanced at the Mel-8704, noticing the Electro Magnetic Force reading red-lining at the same time as the temperature reading registering a substantial drop.

"You're right," Bill said suddenly, fishing in his pocket for the key and handing it to her. "Make sure you lock up when you leave."

She could hear him trudging up the stairs as the meter suddenly returned to normal. But the hairs on the back of her neck had stood up and she shivered and rubbed her arms, trying to shake off the cold feeling.

"Did you feel that?" she asked.

Mark nodded as he sat down on one of the two chairs they had brought into the basement. "I sure did. And did you see Bill's face?"

"Yeah. He looked like he saw a ghost."

A few minutes later, Kathleen radioed upstairs to Angela, notifying her of the readings and Bill's reaction to them. Angela reported nothing except Jacob had been hitting on her. No surprise to Kathleen, as she knew the two, long-time friends had a special chemistry they had chosen not to consummate. Of course, Angela had one year ago divorced her husband of three years due to infidelity, mental and physical abuse. Luckily, there were no kids involved.

And only a month ago, Jacob had discovered something along the same lines. He had found out his girlfriend of three years had visited one of his so-called best friends at his apartment. After they both had become shit-faced, his buddy had told him they had slept in the same bed but nothing had happened. Jacob didn't know what to believe, but he had broken off the union. And, he wasn't sure about a best friend that would even allow his girlfriend to sleep in the same bed with him, even if nothing had happened. Didn't the male protocol call for you to never sleep with your buddy's girlfriend, even if he breaks up with her? Wasn't that an unspoken rule?

At least now they have a bit more in common, Kathleen thought, taking little comfort in the nature of the commonality as she ended the call and set the walkie-talkie down. But, her women's intuition told her Jacob was still smarting from the fresh wound and, if he was wise, would take a few more months to recuperate before jumping into another relationship.

Another two hours passed quietly, except for the creaking of a main-floor door. Jacob had examined the door after the sound and reported there was a problem with one of the hinges that could have caused it to slide open. It was inconclusive.

Kathleen radioed Angela to advise of a location change. She and Mark would be heading upstairs, the other two in the basement. As they exited the small room and walked down the hallway, a low shrieking sound echoed from one of the small rooms at the end of the hallway, perhaps the furnace room.

Kathleen froze to the spot. "Did you hear that?"

"Yeah," Mark said.

"You got the video camera?"

"One of them."

"Let's go."

They slowly walked down the dark hallway, the LED flashlight beams illuminating their passage. They reached the end of the hall, where two doors were closed. One opened into the mechanical room, the other was a storage room. They stopped and listened for what seemed like an eternity.

It was only two minutes.

Suddenly they heard a thumping sound in the storage room that sounded like a book falling off a desk. Kathleen pointed to the door and Mark pushed it open. It creaked on its hinges as it opened.

Both of their eyes widened and their jaws dropped at the ghastly sight in front of them. Mark trained the video camera on the macabre spectacle even though all his instincts told him to run.

Kathleen felt the cold before she saw the apparition. The meter showed a major drop in temperature and a significant rise in EMF. She felt like dropping the meter and hightailing it out of there but, truth be told, she couldn't move if she wanted to.

She was frozen in fear.

Not ten feet in front of them stood a bloodied and battered blonde-haired woman, maybe in her forties—it was hard to tell as her face had been beaten to a pulp with a blunt object and at least half of her skull was caved in, one eye dangling precariously by a thread from one socket. Her disfigured face was covered in blood and her white summer dress was torn and tattered and stained red. She had large gashes along her arms and chest.

Through the hideousness, it appeared she had been attractive in better days. Her body certainly had all the curves in the right places and her ample breasts dangled dangerously close to popping out of the flimsy, bloodied and ripped nightgown. The woman opened her mouth and uttered a loud, painful shriek, followed by a sob.

Kathleen reached for the digital camera, snapped a few pictures as she backed away from the door. Mark backed up with her and continued filming. His recorder suddenly failed. The batteries were dead.

"Fear the chosen one," the woman said suddenly.

"What did you say?" Kathleen asked, trying to will her heart rate to return to normal.

"Fear the chosen one. For he is here and he is evil," the woman said, her mouth contorting in an odd way as she spoke. The blunt force trauma she had suffered had evidently broken her jaw.

"Who is the chosen one?" Kathleen asked, surprised she had become calm enough to ask the question. She could hear footsteps coming down the stairs, knew Jacob and Angela were on route.

The woman opened her mouth to speak but then shrieked, a painful, shrill and helpless sound. Suddenly, she ran out of the storage room, down the hallway, up the stairs and out the door, punctuating her exit by slamming it shut.

"What did you see?" Jacob asked.

"You didn't see anything?" Kathleen asked, feeling the color slowly returning to her face.

Jacob and Angela shook their heads.

"We heard the voices, screams and the door," Angela said. "Felt a cold rush of air on the way down, but didn't see anything." She looked at Jacob for confirmation and he shook his head.

Kathleen looked at Mark, whose face was still an ashen white. "You saw her right Mark?"

He tried to form the words but for a moment nothing came out.

Kathleen felt her heart skip a beat. "Mark, are you okay?"

Finally, he drew a deep breath. "Yeah, I'm okay. And I saw her all right. And we have some of it recorded."

Kathleen was still digesting the way the frightened woman had looked at her as they walked up the stairs toward the main-floor staff cafeteria. They had agreed to take a coffee break, discuss whether they should carry on with the investigation or quit while they were ahead.

Her one eye had a pleading look, like she wants my help, Kathleen thought. She started putting the pieces together. Bill Blythe wasn't Bill Blythe anymore. She was dead sure about that. He had been spewing some religious rhetoric earlier. Bingo. Bill Blythe was the chosen one.

But what was he chosen for?

CHAPTER SIX

"I'm the chosen one."

"You're what?" Thelma asked, munching on chips and channel-surfing. A tea table sat in front of her with a lone can of Coke. She reclined her bulk on a worn-out but comfortable brown armchair, her legs stretched out on a yellow leather footstool, grey duct tape on one corner only partially concealing a large rip.

"I'm the chosen one," James Maling said through the raspy vocal cords of Bill Blythe.

"Would you quit talking nonsense and get me another bag of chips from the kitchen," she said, finally deciding on a war movie and setting the remote control on the tea table.

Objects slowly appeared in the blank white space in Bill Blythe's mind and it took a few seconds for him to register his whereabouts. *What the hell just happened? Oh, I better not use that word. Did I blank out? Is this the first time? No. What happened Saturday night? I don't know. And a few nights before that? I remember when I got home, but not much before. Shit, this isn't good.*

He blinked and registered his rotund wife glaring at him, strands of her long grey hair popping out in comical directions. She had yet to visit with her hair brush. Her white sweatshirt was stained brown in spots and speckled with chip crumbs. Bits of chewed chips stuck to the corners of her wrinkled mouth.

Did she just say something?

"Did you hear me, or did you go all stupid on me?" she asked.

"I can't remember what you said."

"Oh, here we go. First you start talking a bunch of nonsense, now you can't remember what I said. Let's do this again. I said, shut your pie hole and get me some chips from the kitchen. Is that rocket science?"

He felt his cheeks flush as he stood up from the couch, walked into the kitchen and returned with a bag of chips, handing them to her before sitting down.

She grunted, tearing the bag open and continuing to feed.

It was a Sunday afternoon, and the two sat in the Blythe residence, a hundred-year-old brick two-story home on Durham Street. Bill squirmed on the couch, feeling more and more restless the more he thought about his black-outs, or blank-outs, depending on your perspective. Bursts of machine gun fire and bombs exploded from the movie on the television and Thelma loudly crunched her potato chips, the odd crumb falling on her sweatshirt. Bill was oblivious to it.

He only knew that, when he glanced at her, he was filled with an emotion he had up to this point in his life been largely unfamiliar with. But, now the emotion—RAGE—wanted an intimate relationship with him.

The hot anger started in his stomach and crept up through his body into recesses of his mind he had thought long dormant. His cheeks flushed and his fingers dug into couch fabric as he tried to stop his blood from boiling over. *Should I go over and smack her in the head? Get that thought out of your mind. You know she deserves it. Forget it, forget it, forget it.*

He felt like he would explode at any second if he didn't do something. His relationship with Thelma had become contemptuously familiar. He dared not think about it right now. He knew with certainty if he did, he would no longer be responsible for his actions. *Do something, you idiot.*

No longer able to contain the rage threatening to gush out swiftly like a hot and steamy geyser bubbling over during a volcanic eruption, he stood and walked to the front door.

"Don't forget to take out the garbage," Thelma said.

His face reddened and turned a purplish color. His eyes bulged. He balled his fists, briefly unclenched his right hand just long enough to open the door, step out onto the porch and quietly close it behind him. He took five steps down his concrete walkway, raised his fists to the sky and shouted, "Why meeeeeeeeeee?"

Reverend James Maling squinted at the sun, looked at his fists and wondered what he was doing as a passing motorist shot him a surprised look. Then he remembered it was Sunday. *Right. There must be an afternoon mass at the local church. I'm sure I can find some souls that need saving.*

CHAPTER SEVEN

Kathleen walked along Main Street, Montague, on a clear bright Wednesday afternoon trying to make sense of the events of last Saturday night. The horrific image of the bloodied and battered woman had frightened her and after their short coffee break, the team had decided to pack it in and head home. They had had enough fun for one night.

Jacob and Angela had wanted to stay, but part of the team credo was if after a significant incident one of them wanted to go, they all went. It was the protocol. So, at Kathleen's urging, they had packed up and left.

She didn't realize she could become so scared, nor that the feeling of dread would last for so long. In her years as a paranormal investigator, she had been poked and prodded by ghosts and had felt fear. But nothing came close to the raw terror she had experienced that night. After they had dropped off Jacob and Angela, they arrived at her apartment, where they had discussed the events for a few hours before finally deciding to turn in for the night.

Kathleen had tossed for most of the night before finally falling into a restless sleep. She had a nightmare that Bill Blythe was attacking the battered woman with a large metal shovel, beating her repeatedly to more of a pulp than she had already been beaten. The dream was also sexual in nature. It seemed the woman had been raped and then murdered, but now the details were all muddled in her mind and she couldn't remember. She woke up afraid, drenched in sweat and walked into the bathroom, while Mark slept comfortably, to splash some cold water on her face.

That's when she saw and heard her office door down the hall creak open. She lived on the third floor of a 130-year-old brick building and she had never seen that door move like that before. She had walked down the hall to check it and felt a cold rush of air as she pushed it closed. Too scared to investigate further, and not wanting to wake up Mark who she knew was exhausted, she had retreated to bed where she had spent the remainder of the night awake and tossing uncomfortably.

That Sunday, she had told Mark she needed a few days to recover before analyzing the recordings. She had wanted to think about other things. She didn't bother telling him about the door, deciding it could wait until she felt better.

What had been bothering her, and still bothered her now as she walked up Queens Road on her way to Dr. Heeling's office, was an edge that she was beginning to feel, a sort of anxiousness and stress she felt was the precursor to another anxiety attack. What made it worse was the edge was accompanied by thoughts of imminent danger on the horizon, a feeling that something was very wrong. It had been exactly those thoughts, but much more intense, that had been symptomatic of her first anxiety attack.

What should have made her feel better, but didn't, was when Mark had announced Sunday afternoon while they sat on a bench at Viking Park that he would be receiving a cash settlement for his back injury and wanted to buy a house where they both could live. She had smiled at the time, hugged him tightly and kissed him long and full on the lips, but she couldn't help wondering if she was really fit to cohabitate with anyone.

A week ago, she would have been jumping up and down with glee. But, it wasn't a week ago anymore now.

She turned up the walkway to the historic professional building where Dr. Heeling had his office, pulled open the big glass door and went inside. She notified the receptionist of her arrival, sat down, picked up a magazine and started anxiously flipping through the pages, not bothering to read anything. She looked at pictures and it took her five or so minutes to realize she had a Maclean's news magazine in her hands.

An old man who sat across from her suddenly gasped for breath, stopped breathing for a moment and began taking deep breaths.

"Are you okay?" Kathleen asked. She was qualified to do CPR and was about to start administering it before she noticed his labored breathing had returned to normal. She was sure he was about to have a heart attack right in front of her. *Where have I seen him before?*

"Better than ever," the man said through bloodshot eyes. His hair was matted to one side like he had just woke up and his grey suit was wrinkled. He sported more than a four o'clock shadow. It was at least a five-day growth. "I was at afternoon mass on Sunday. I'm a chosen one now."

Kathleen's eyes bulged and she wiped her arms, trying to obliterate the crop of goose bumps that had instantly sprouted.

"Miss Freeborne." the receptionist said. "The doctor will see you now."

About fifteen minutes later, Dr. Heeling studied some papers as if it were there he would find the solution to Kathleen's anxiety attacks. As clearly as possible, she had explained the attack and the edge she felt. He sat studying the papers through horn-rimmed glasses, occasionally running his hand through a thick mop of grey hair. He looked like Albert Einstein.

Kathleen wondered if perhaps he painted for a hobby or maybe he was a fiction writer. Although he was a man of science, his appearance and demeanor very much resembled that of an artist. He had been her family doctor for the last decade and she liked him. She felt he really cared for his patients, instead of just cycling them through his office like her last doctor did, trying to cram in as many billable hours in a day as possible.

"Have you been feeling depressed at all?" he asked, pulling off the glasses and wiping his eyes as he regarded her curiously.

"No. I feel a little anxious sometimes, and I tend to worry. But I've never had any prolonged bouts of depression."

"Well, we know you don't have any serious symptoms of depression in your past. At least none that you've shared with me. But what about recently?"

"No," Kathleen said. "My life is going well for the most part. I have a good relationship, good job, goals. I'm happy." She decided, at least for now, she would leave out the experience at the theatre, even though he knew she was a paranormal investigator. If they were going to go there, it would be on his initiative only.

"Let's talk about your job for a minute," Heeling said, setting his glasses on the papers. "A rather stressful job, teaching autistic children. Can you think of any incidents at work? Triggers maybe, that might have caused your attack?"

Kathleen paused. She didn't want to tell him about control freak Ron Baglund either. It was a small community and word through the gossip grapevine travelled lightning fast. If you started bad-mouthing people around here, it wasn't long before your reputation was trashed. She knew only too well the unspoken rules of living in a small town. And, although she thought she could trust Dr. Heeling, she wasn't prepared to extend that trust into her workplace.

For all she knew, Baglund was a patient, or worse, a friend of Heeling's.

"No," she finally said. "We get kids who act up sometimes, but I've been doing this for a while and I've always been able to handle it professionally."

"And you still can?" he asked.

"I think so."

He seemed convinced. There was a moment's pause, before he finally said, "I think we need to start you on medication."

"Medication? I've never taken medication," Kathleen said, immediately feeling stupid for saying it. She had already mentioned the edge to him and what it meant. She instinctively knew where he would go next.

"Well, could you imagine," he said, "If you were to have an anxiety attack at work, how that might put your professional life in jeopardy?"

"I get it," she said. "What medication did you have in mind?"

"Zoloft is an anti-depressant that is also used to treat anxiety and panic disorders. I've had good success on other patients with it."

"How long before it starts working?"

"It might take a week to twelve days before you have enough of it built up in your system to start taking effect. And, it might not work at all. We might have to try you on a few different drugs before we get it right. It's the nature of the disorder."

Kathleen sighed. "What are the side effects?"

"I'll give you some printed material," the doctor said, pulling out two sheets from the stack of papers on his desk. Maybe the answer was in the papers after all. "But you might have anxiety, agitation, aggressiveness, hostility, depression, mood swings and physical symptoms such as muscle stiffness, fever, nausea, headache, trouble sleeping and a few more."

"That's a lot," Kathleen said.

"We'll try you on it. There are less serious side effects like drowsiness, decreased appetite, decreased sex drive and mild fatigue. All the serious side effects are listed here," he said, standing and handing her the papers. "If you have any one of them I want you to call me immediately, okay?"

"Sure," Kathleen said, feeling like a human guinea pig for the pharmaceutical industry.

Walking out of the office with a prescription, she couldn't help but notice the old man in the waiting room who she was sure had stopped breathing earlier, was now uttering some incomprehensible chant. He stopped as she passed, stared at her wide-eyed and said, "You need to be saved, young lady."

She did her best to ignore the comment and left the office.

A few minutes later, after filling the prescription and dry-swallowing one of the pills, she walked into the small classroom at the school.

She went over to Dylan, her nine-year-old star pupil. He had just sat down at his work station, put on a set of headphones and was listening to music. His eyes floated dreamily around the room as he listened. He smiled as he noticed her approach. With a hand that was not quite steady, she slowly lifted the headset from his head and set it on the desk.

"We're going to start your math exercise now," Kathleen said.

He grunted and gave her a warm smile.

Dylan, a cute boy with short blonde hair and intelligent blue eyes, was not unlike many autistic children suffering from the neurological disorder. He was very bright but his social interaction and communication were impaired. Left unattended, his mind would drift off in many different directions and he would be unable to complete his exercises. He needed specialized and individual attention so he might one day lead a normal life. Autism sufferers needed to have structured days and they needed teachers that can be firm but gentle at the same time.

He reached for the headset—a diversion for him during breaks—and Kathleen placed a hand on his arm. "No, Dylan. That's for later. Let's finish your math. It's here, on the computer screen, look."

His eyes darted around the room momentarily, looked one more time at the head-phones, then returned to the computer screen.

Kathleen noticed the two other educational assistants busy with their students. Her colleague, Linda Wellington, flashed a warm smile and she returned it before carrying on with the exercises. There were a total of six students in the small classroom, each with a fully equipped and high-tech work station. Four staff—three educational assistants and a teacher—worked there.

Ron Baglund had yet to return from his lunch break. It seemed he ran his own schedule and came and went at random. When she had first met him two years ago, her gut told her he was a bit of an odd ball, to say the least. Since that time, she had also heard, through the lightning-fast local grapevine, that he was a recluse with anti-social tendencies.

None of it surprised her. She almost expected him to walk in at any time and start freaking out.

Like clockwork, the diminutive teacher with the comb-over, nerd glasses and self-assured smile strode into the room with a few files, a cursory nod of acknowledgement to the assistants, and sat down at his desk. He was a stubby little guy of maybe five feet.

Maybe he has Napoleon complex, Kathleen wondered, as Dylan solved one math equation after the other. "Very good," she said. "I wish I was as good at math as you are."

He smiled. "Goo?" That's how he said good.

"Yes, you're very good. Very smart."

Ron walked over to Kathleen, regarding her wearily. "Is everything okay here?"

"Fine, just fine."

She wondered how long before news of her anxiety attack would make its way into the classroom. She doubted the pharmacist who had filled her prescription, eyeballing her knowingly, would strictly follow the confidentiality policies governing her profession. It was only a matter of time.

"I'd like to talk to you after work," he said.

"Me?"

"Yes, you. Do I look like I'm talking to someone else?"

"No problem," she said, not wanting to provoke another outburst. She didn't know what had set him off today, but she suspected he was still dwelling on the recent incident involving the autistic student Irene, who had thrown a violent temper tantrum recently.

He walked over to the other assistants, had short conversations with them and returned to his desk. Linda rolled her eyes at Kathleen as he busied himself with some papers and Kathleen knew the after-work meeting would involve the other assistants as well. *We're in for a group tongue-lashing. But at least this time he's not going to do it in front of the children.*

Two hours later it was just as Kathleen had thought. The three assistants sat around Ron's desk and he shuffled some papers, placed them neatly to one side, and looked sternly from one face to the next.

"Okay, maybe I didn't make it clear last time, but there's a way that I want this classroom run. And it's my way. If we ever have a problem like Irene's recent temper tantrum, I do not, I repeat do not under any circumstances want you to call Child Welfare Services." He regarded the faces seriously. No one spoke.

"Kathleen, why did you and your colleagues see fit to call child welfare?"

It probably doesn't matter how I answer. I'll get shit anyway. "Mr. Baglund (he preferred that to his first name), it wasn't us who made the decision. Irene went into a complete rage. We couldn't reach her parents, so the principal made the call. We couldn't reach you either." Kathleen knew something about control freaks. And what she had learned from a domineering ex-boyfriend was give them the control and they don't know what to do with it. She had said the wrong thing and she was going to pay. There was no doubt about it.

"I don't care about any of that stuff," Ron said. "You do not consult other staff, you consult me. And only me. Is this clear?"

"I'm sorry, Mr. Baglund. I made the wrong call. And I promise it won't happen again." *That's better. Let's see what he does with that one. I wonder if he knows about my anxiety attack?*

"It better not happen again, young lady, or there will be hell to pay."

Kathleen mustered her best chastised look and sat silently, looking down at her hands while he shifted his attention to the other two assistants, Linda Wellington and Becky Johnson. It seemed as though they had learned something from Kathleen's apology because their stories differed only marginally. Linda just straight-up offered an apology, saying she had seriously erred in judgment and would make sure it never happened again.

After a short lecture on classroom protocol, he dismissed the group. Kathleen noticed his cheeks were flushed red with anger. He looked as though he was about to pop. He had expected them to mount a vigorous defense of their actions so he would have the opportunity rip them to pieces.

As it was, he would have to vent his anger somewhere else. Kathleen smiled as she walked down the hall. Just as she was about to descend the stairs to the exit, she heard a faint stomping sound from Ron's office. It was followed by a litany of muffled profanity.

CHAPTER EIGHT

"I just have a bad feeling," Kathleen said.

"What does it tell you?" Mark asked.

"Something is definitely wrong with Bill Blythe. I think he's possessed and whatever's inside of him wants to inflict serious damage here."

"I wouldn't use that term loosely," Mark said. He strived to be as scientific as possible in his paranormal investigations and tried to steer clear of religious terminology. He knew other paranormal investigators wouldn't necessarily agree with him but also knew it was hard to find consensus among the paranormal community on paranormal definitions anyway.

"I'm not using it loosely," Kathleen said. As much as she loved her man, she thought him too rigid in his thought process at times. They had discussed Bill's unusual behavior the night at the theatre, his religious ramblings and the battered apparition warning them to beware of the chosen one. For good measure, she had thrown in the story about the old man in the doctor's office, another chosen one, telling her she needed saving. The last thing she mentioned was her office door creaking open, and the possibility a ghost had followed her home and was now cohabitating with her.

Mark had been around the paranormal long enough not to dismiss anything she had said. He just wasn't a huge fan of religion, so disliked religious labels like possession. But truth be told, when he stayed in his own home, he slept with the light on. He knew only too well what strange things stirred at night.

"What do you want to do?" he sighed.

"Why don't we do some internet searching?" They often helped clients by doing a historical analysis of properties. In one investigation, residents of a house had distinctly heard the ghost say his name, John, followed by "Get out of this house." A month later during their research, they discovered that a man by the name of John had been brutally murdered on the property and he apparently didn't want anyone around. The team had tried to convince John to leave during follow-up investigations but a few weeks later, the client called and said ghost John had tried to strangle her in the middle of the night.

Traumatized, the couple had packed their bags and left the next day.

As far as Kathleen knew, the house was still vacant. In record time, the gossip grapevine had delivered the news the house was haunted and now nobody would go near it.

Mark sat beside her as she tapped some keys on her computer and eventually accessed Library and Archives Canada. A few minutes later, she smiled. "This is it," she said. "Look."

They slid their chairs closer to the computer monitor and read.

The story, an excerpt from a newspaper dated 1856, told how Georgetown resident Elizabeth Pelletier was brutally raped and bludgeoned to death and her body dumped on the banks of the Montague River, close to the town.

What was interesting about the story was what had happened the day before her death. Apparently Elizabeth, a single mother of 45, didn't take kindly to a Reverend James Maling, who had declared his family were the chosen people of God and anyone who did not agree with his vision was in serious jeopardy of losing their souls to the Devil.

According to the report, during one of Maling's sermons in church, Elizabeth took exception to his holier-than-thou attitude. She stood up and declared all people were created equal in the eyes of God and that his vision was more than just false. It was blasphemous.

There was a hushed silence in the congregation as Elizabeth stormed out. It was rumored that Maling, after she left, had said, "She has sealed her fate with the Devil."

During the police investigation, a grubbing hoe was found to be the murder weapon. Although it belonged to the Maling family, James Maling was subsequently tried for the murder and acquitted. No one had ever been charged after that.

Kathleen's eyes widened as she comprehended the full weight of the story. A glimpse of her nightmare flashed into her head and she remembered seeing something about rape. It was beginning to add up. "The ghost we saw is Elizabeth Pelletier," she said.

"And Bill Blythe is possessed by James Maling," Mark said.

"What do we do?" Kathleen asked, her heart beginning to race. She felt a little drowsy from the medication but the recent discovery was rapidly clearing out the cobwebs.

"I'd like to see if we can determine where they were buried," Mark said.

"We can do that later," Kathleen said, glancing at the clock: 7:15pm. She did a quick Google search, pulling up Bill Blythe's address on Durham Street. She scribbled it on a piece of paper, grabbed her jacket while running down the hallway to the entrance door. "Let's go, Mark. Let's do a drive-by and see what's happening at the Blythe residence."

Fifteen minutes later, they sat in Black Death outside Bill Blythe's home. The night was frosty but clear and the stars and moon illuminated the street, along with the streetlights. The snow remaining from the recent storm also helped with visibility, reflecting the moonlight. Kathleen peered in the bay window through a pair of binoculars. "Look, he's at the window," she said, handing Mark the binoculars. He peered through them and nodded.

"He's closing the curtains," Kathleen said. "What should we do?"

"What can we do?" Mark handed her back the binoculars.

"We have to do something. What if his wife's in danger?"

"Do you want me to call Detective Redmond and tell him we have a possessed man who's going to kill someone?"

Yeah, right, she thought. "Let's go up and knock on the door."

"And say what?"

"I don't know. That we just wanted to make sure he's okay because he seemed out of sorts the other night."

There was a pause while they both pondered the idea. Did they have a better plan? Probably not. They looked at each other, nodded and simultaneously stepped out of Black Death. Kathleen led the way as they walked up the shoveled walkway leading to the character Victorian-style home. Mark double-checked his cell phone, satisfied the detective was still on speed-dial. Just in case.

They exchanged puzzled glances as Kathleen rang the doorbell. "That sounded like a muffled scream," she whispered.

Mark nodded, the color draining from his face. Kathleen buzzed again. Nothing.

Then they heard the thumping sounds of a struggle coming from within the house and faintly, "Help ... me."

"We have to do something," Kathleen whispered urgently.

Mark tried the door. It was unlocked, much like many doors in this small community where crime, violent or otherwise, was a rarity. He pushed it open and they gasped at the sight in front of them.

Bill Blythe leaned over Thelma, both hands choking her forcefully. Her mouth hung open and she gasped for air unsuccessfully. Her face had turned purple and her eyes bulged in their sockets. Bill turned his head, acknowledging them with a smile.

The life drained from Thelma.

"This bitch is finally getting what she deserves," he snarled, returning his gaze to Thelma.

Mark handed his phone to Kathleen. "Speed-dial Redmond. Number 4." He rushed across the living room, tackling Bill, sending him crashing into the wall, knocking over a lamp and breaking it. He mounted him, pinned him down and held him. Bill's aging body was no match for the youthful strength of Mark.

Bill's wild eyes slowly returned to normal. "What are you doing here?" he asked Mark, blinking. "Why are you in my house?"

Kathleen had called Redmond and urgently given the detective their address; then ran over to Thelma and propped her up in the chair. She coughed, gasped and spit. The color slowly returned to her weathered features.

She had come very close to death.

CHAPTER NINE

"Is death really that bad?" PEIPI team member Jacob asked himself, the hot water cascading off his body as he showered Thursday morning in his small one-bedroom apartment on the second floor of an old four-unit building on the corner of Main Street and MacDonald Avenue.

Get that thought out of your mind. The black cloud will disappear. It just takes time.

Since his union with his ex-girlfriend Lisa had ended, just over a month ago now, he still found himself thinking of her often. He tried hard to flush the thoughts from his mind but inevitably they would creep back in. Most of the images involved her delectable body while a few of them had to do with some of the good times they had shared as a couple.

The thoughts that inevitably churned around the images had to do with her lying to him about her undying loyalty. They had been together for three years; that she would strip her clothes off—shit-faced or not—and climb into the same bed as his so-called friend Steve continued to haunt and upset him. Steve had even mentioned that although he wasn't completely sure—he too was out of his tree at the time—he thought she had kissed him before falling asleep.

What else did they do before she fell asleep?

He had seen Steve socially a few times after the incident, but all that did was remind him of Lisa. And when Steve left, the black cloud in his head would grow. For the past month, Jacob would wake feeling okay, if a little flat and unenthused about life. He would feel a small black cloud of depression in his temple, just slightly behind the scenes—but ready to attack when the opportunity presented itself. As the day wore on, it would grow in intensity and by mid-afternoon would render him incapable of functioning normally.

He worked from his apartment as a website designer so fortunately when the black cloud reached an unbearable size, usually by mid-afternoon, he would turn the phones off and take a nap on the couch. He found sleep would wash away the physical pain in his head and when he woke he was usually feeling well enough to carry on working until the late hours of the evening, delaying sleep for as long as possible.

The cloud would reappear later in the night, just before bed, but with much less intensity and he found he could usually manage it. But last night had been an exception. Images of Lisa's body had clouded his mind and he had tossed and turned for over an hour before finally drifting off.

He dreamed he was with a bunch of friends partying and Lisa was somewhere in the background talking and drinking with some people. Maybe they were at a house party, he couldn't be sure. He remembered approaching her and asking her to join him. He was met by a cold shoulder. He approached her later in the dream with the same invitation and had been greeted by her smile, which he found so attractive and sexy. However on the third approach, she had turned her back to him, frowning as she swiveled around in her chair.

He had woken up rattled, and lay in bed tossing for an hour or so before finally falling asleep. But when he finally awoke at 10:06 am to begin his work day, he found images of the dream were fresh in his mind and he thought the tiny black cloud's progress would be a lot swifter today.

His rational mind told him he was just going through a mourning period, common for any break-up, and he should try and extract the positives from the experience and learn from them to become a better person. And, he had to admit, some days, particularly when he was with his friend Angela, the black cloud had completely disappeared. But he also knew, as much as he was tempted by her body and her mind, it was probably too soon for both of them to begin a new relationship. They were mourning their losses. And Angela had become such a good friend that Jacob wasn't sure he wanted to change the dynamic of their relationship, as much as he thought they had a lot on common and would make a great couple.

He had thought of talking to a counselor to help him cope, but something told him that talking about the painful experience would only give it life and make it more painful. So he had resisted, hoping that time, the great healer, would eventually erase his painful memories.

He had also resisted medication of any sort, with only one exception: alcohol. He had gone on two benders, drinking beer late into the night. It was true that while he was wasted the black cloud had completely disappeared, but it was also true that when he had woke up the next day, his head pounding with a hangover, the cloud had enveloped his mind swiftly, with such ferocity and debilitating effects it had frightened him.

He was about to step out of the shower when an image of Lisa's naked body crept into his mind. He stepped back into the tub, turned the water on full and remained five or so more minutes, hoping the hot, wet stream cascading off his head would wash away the hurtful memories. It didn't. But, he thought, as he dried himself: *It helped a little.*

He approached his image in the mirror as he towel-dried his hair. He sported a crew cut and liked it. No, muss, no fuss. Towel dry and good to go, nothing even long enough to comb. His expression was blank, his green eyes giving away perhaps a little sadness. *Not that noticeable though. And most people are so preoccupied with their own shit they wouldn't notice.*

He dressed, walked into his office which was also his kitchen table, and sat down to work. His thoughts drifted to the investigation at the theatre and he started to realize how much it had really scared him. The team had yet to analyze the data but he knew one thing for sure; he hadn't seen anything but he knew damn well what he had heard. The clearly audible shrieking and talking had put a fright in him like no other investigation. He thought of calling Angela, but then realized she would be at her cashier job at Sobeys and wouldn't be able to answer the phone. He also thought of walking the few blocks to visit her but he didn't like that idea either. He had work to do.

The voices from the theatre crept into his head again. Well, better that than an image of Lisa's desirable body. He was also disturbed about the recent news regarding Bill Blythe and his wife Thelma. Allegedly, he'd tried to murder her and was now in police custody. He tried to push those thoughts from his mind and went to work on his latest project, building a website for an upstart author who wanted desperately to begin earning some money from the two books he had just published.

Three hours later the black cloud had grown to a painful and unmanageable level. But he had been able to get a lot of web design accomplished. He longed for the day when the ache's pervasive and detrimental force would disappear forever. He lay down and drifted off in a matter of minutes. At least he was able to sleep in the afternoons since the black cloud also sapped his energy.

A few hours later, he was awakened by his cell phone ringing. He had forgotten to turn it off. The black cloud did that sometimes. It made you forget things. He looked at the clock: 6:53 pm. He had slept for longer than he wanted to. Rubbing his eyes, he saw Angela's number and smiled—something he hadn't done a lot of lately.

"Hi," he said.

"How are you?"

"I'm okay." It was mutually understood that, right now, *they* were not okay though. They had touched on their mutual heartbreak only briefly in the past and then let it alone, like an unspoken rule that some things were better left unsaid. He didn't ask pointed questions and either did she. "And you?"

"Not so well."

"What happened?"

"I was in the shower and I heard the bathroom door open and suddenly the room became very cold. It freaked me out. Especially after what happened the other night."

"Who was it?"

"I don't know. There's no one in the house right now. Only me."

"Do you want me to come over?"

"I was hoping you would. I'm a little scared. I might call Mark and Kathleen."

CHAPTER TEN

Mark and Kathleen sat comfortably on a couch in Kathleen's apartment watching the local news, looking for a report on Bill Blythe.

Detective Redmond had arrived at the Blythe household a few minutes after Kathleen had made the panicked phone call and found Mark sitting on Bill Blythe's chest. After the detective had asked a few preliminary questions, and noticed the large red welts on Thelma's neck, Bill had been handcuffed, put into a separate cop car, arrested for attempted murder and taken into custody.

He had looked absolutely shocked the entire time, like he had no idea of what had just happened.

A few minutes later the two had taken a backseat in Redmond's car and he had asked them some questions. Kathleen had explained her theory about Bill being possessed by a priest who had probably been buried beneath the theatre some time back in the early 1800s. Even as she had told the story, she had remembered thinking to herself how ridiculous it sounded.

Redmond had looked at them skeptically the entire time and, after a half hour or so, dismissed them from his vehicle, reminding them they would be called upon at some point to testify. He had also reminded Mark the police planned on proceeding with charges against Die-Yodeler (of course he didn't call her that) and wanted his testimony on that case as well.

In the last few days, Kathleen had noticed the medication had brought down the edge of her anxiety a little, but she still felt it just below the surface and had her doubts about whether it would work in the long run. She had also spoken to one of her friends on the phone who had suffered from panic attacks. Apparently Melissa was having good success for the past two years, with limited side effects, taking a medication called Thorazine. She had also advised Kathleen on limiting sugar intake, caffeine, getting the proper amount of exercise and sleep.

For the time being, anyway, her resident ghost had disappeared. But she was not able to locate any gravestones for Elizabeth or James. Which didn't rule out the possibility they had been buried underneath the theatre and not exhumed prior to construction.

Her cell phone rang and she jerked her head, startled. It had caught her off-guard, like cell phones do sometimes. She saw Angela's number and picked it up. "Hi, how are you?"

"Not so good. Jacob just got over here. Could you guys come over? I had my bathroom door mysteriously open while I was in the shower and I'm scared."

"We'll be right there," she said, making a face to Mark indicating a PEIPI member needed their help.

"Bring some equipment," Angela said.

As they walked out the door, Kathleen wondered why she hadn't thought to set up any of the recording equipment in her own apartment.

About five minutes later, Black Death pulled in front of Angela's turn-of-the-century brick two-story home on Hillcrest Avenue. Mark grabbed the duffle bag of equipment while Kathleen walked up to the house and rang the doorbell. Angela had inherited the home from her grandfather and at one time had lived in it with her ex-husband, Aaron. When they split, she got her house.

Angela answered the door in a yellow nightgown. Her blonde hair was disheveled, her blue eyes slightly bloodshot. She had had better days.

Kathleen hugged her and sat down in the living room next to Jacob. Mark began setting up the recording devices. Jacob stood up, grabbed a Mel-8704 and walked into the bathroom.

"Are you okay?" Kathleen asked, when Angela sat down.

"It just freaked me out, but I'm fine." She looked far from fine. "I was in the shower ... I heard the bathroom door creak open, the room suddenly got very cold and I got scared. I jumped out of the shower, screamed and threw my robe on."

Kathleen told her about her office door opening a few days ago and Angela sighed.

"I'm getting something in here," Jacob said from the bathroom.

Mark, who had just finished setting up audio and video recorders, plucked a Mel-8704 from the duffle bag and went into the bathroom.

The readings on both meters spiked with electro-magnetic energy. The room became colder and the meter registered the temperature change. Kathleen picked up one of the audio-video tripods Mark had left in the living room and carried it into the bathroom. She also brought a digital camera in and snapped a few pictures.

Angela remained on the armchair. It was a small bathroom after all.

A few minutes later the readings returned to normal—whatever that was—and the team exchanged puzzled glances, before returning to the living room.

They were good friends and they chatted amicably. Jacob talked of his latest website development project, Mark told an animated story of the tenant from hell, Angela relayed an interesting story about an old man wandering through the supermarket calling himself the chosen one and touching other patrons as he passed them.

Kathleen, for her part, told the story of control freak Baglund finally getting control and not having a clue what to do with it.

Underneath the surface of the conversation, Kathleen couldn't help but notice a tension among the group, a tension that had not been there before. Something had changed since their visit to the King's Playhouse and, while she dreaded the thought, she wasn't sure any of their lives would ever be the same again. She hoped she was wrong but something told her she was very right.

"That guy in Sobeys," she said, looking at Angela. "Did he have a grey, wrinkled suit? Matted hair?"

Angela nodded, her dazed eyes becoming focused.

"It's the same guy I saw in the doctor's office," Kathleen said. "He told me I need to be saved. It freaked me out." She hadn't bothered to tell Angela and Jacob why she was in the doctor's office and they hadn't bothered to ask. Of course, Mark knew. But he was entitled. *People need to have certain things private. True friends respect that.*

Kathleen couldn't help connecting all the dots to Reverend James Maling and she wondered what he was up to. But, at the same time, with all the crazy shit that had gone on lately, and her precarious mental state, feeling near the edge, she wasn't sure she could intelligently draw a connection between Maling, Elizabeth, and the new chosen one who had just appeared on the scene, proselytizing.

Why not? Why can't you draw a connection? It's right there in front of you.

Suddenly the vibe in the room became very dark and Kathleen noticed Mark and Jacob's expressions had soured.

What's going on here?

She stood up and felt a dark force—black and evil was how she would later describe it—pass right through her body. It frightened her so much, draining her energy at the same time, that she slumped back onto the couch.

"I just felt a very dark presence," she said, wide-eyed.

They all started simultaneously as the audio-video recorder in the bathroom came crashing down, the lens shattering, shards of glass sweeping out into the living room and across the rustic hardwood floor.

"What the fuck," Mark said, as he stood up with his meter.

Suddenly a voice, loud, deep and authoritative, reverberated through the room: "Get out of here now!"

There was a long pause as the group waited, wanting to see if more instructions would come. A few seconds passed and nothing happened. Mark went into the bathroom.

Kathleen could feel the tiny hairs on her back stand up as her boyfriend left. She could also feel the edge as the blackness exited her body and wondered for how long she would be mentally fit to investigate the paranormal.

"Could you please tell us your name and why you want us to leave?" Mark asked.

They all waited, letting Mark take control. He was the group's founder and a certain amount of respect was necessary. In some previous investigations, he had asked questions of ghosts and received answers. During one outing, he had repeatedly asked a ghost to rattle a door to signal his presence and the ghost had willingly complied, right on cue. He was methodical and calm when dealing with the paranormal and that meant he could sometimes solicit a response.

But not this time. He asked variations of the same question for perhaps five minutes and nothing happened. And the group waited an extra fifteen or so minutes in complete silence. Nothing.

Kathleen looked at the clock finally as they all sat around nervously. They had been trained not to become nervous, but it wasn't working. "It's almost midnight," she said. "I think we should call it a night."

"Are you okay to stay here tonight?" Jacob asked a white-faced Angela.

"I don't know," Angela said. Actually she did know. She wanted desperately to have Jacob stay with her overnight. She was very frightened. But there was something not right about his eyes. He didn't look like her friend Jacob anymore. His expression told her he would just as soon slit her throat as take care of her. "I'll be okay," she said without conviction.

After some discussion, the team decided to set up an audio-video camera in Angela's bedroom and a separate audio recorder.

On the way home, Kathleen realized that things had gone from bad to worse. Mark had given her some strange, dark looks in Angela's house, which she was trying hard to comprehend. The evil force that had passed through her had left her with trembling hands. She absently put them in her pockets, hoping it would stop the shaking.

The edge was snapping at her mind, wanting to come out to play.

CHAPTER ELEVEN

Angela sat on the edge of her bed, fluffed up her pillow and laid down. She couldn't shake the weird expression Jacob had given her before he had departed, as though he would relish the thought of doing nasty and cruel things to her. There was something in his eyes that she had never noticed before, some unfathomable evil lying in wait.

She reached over, turned her nightstand light off, shifted around trying to find a comfortable position. The room was dark, but for the small blue streaks of moonlight shining through the bamboo curtain and the red glowing light that told her the video camera was filming her every move.

She had hesitated when Jacob had asked her if she was okay. In reality, she felt very *not* okay. She wanted to ask Jacob to stay the night, or at least spend the night at his apartment. But the nasty look had prevented it. The look had scared her and made her nervous about wanting to spend an extended period of time with those eyes.

Should I call him? Maybe it was just my imagination. Should I call him, ask if I can come over? No. Better not. It's getting late. Maybe I should call Aaron? Are you nuts, girl? Don't even think of calling him.

Angela tried to force the thought of her ex from her mind as she turned over, finally finding a comfortable position stretched out on her back, staring at the ceiling. If she had any flaws in her character, they were related to being too nice. She had let herself put up with Aaron's physical and mental abuse for three years too long before finally finding the courage to leave him. And if it hadn't been for her one-time best friend Melina Tamble deciding to sleep with Aaron, she would probably still be with him. In retrospect, she figured Melina had probably done her a favor, knocking on the door of her house while she was out on an all-night paranormal investigation and seducing her ex-husband.

Part of the problem was Angela lacked self-esteem and confidence. To be loved, regardless of the character of the lover, had been reason enough to stay with him. The other problem was that Aaron wasn't all bad. He had a good, loving and caring side that, when she first met him at the supermarket, seemed like the dominant part of his personality.

But after getting married and moving in with him, things slowly began to deteriorate. It seemed he wanted to know her every move and tried to keep her confined to the house as much as possible, discouraging her from developing friendships, socializing and even pursuing extra-curricular activities like painting, which she loved so much.

His abuse was very subtle. He would make remarks about her intelligence. "Can't you think your way through that one?" And subtle comments about her appearance: "Can't you do something different with your hair?" Or, "Do you have to wear that shirt?"

And, except for one time when he had hauled off and back-handed her in the head, sending her crashing into a wall, his physical abuse had started off somewhat subtly. He would usually grab her by the arm firmly when he didn't want her to do something, pull her gently wherever he wanted her to land, sometimes forcing her to sit down. But, eventually the physical contact grew fiercer and more aggressive, to the point where she often had black hand-print bruises on both arms that never seemed to heal.

It was the slow, increasing intensity of the abuse that had gradually crept up on her. The comments slowly eroded her confidence and self-esteem to the point where she almost thought she deserved everything Aaron said and did to her. But Kathleen had helped her see things for what they were. Kathleen had told her she was in an extremely unhealthy relationship and should get out of it soon. That she was beautiful, special, could do better than Aaron. The thought, like a small seedling, had lingered, slowly taken root and started to grow. Of course the catalyst was the infidelity, the proverbial straw that broke the camel's back.

After the infidelity, when she finally found the courage to tell Aaron to leave the matrimonial house, it was Kathleen who had waited outside in her car, ready to call the cops if there was any hint of violence. And it was Kathleen who, when Aaron began protesting and applied a vice-like grip to Angela's arms, had walked into the house, clicked open her cell phone, saying, "You had better get your ass out of this house now before I call the police. I know what's been happening around here."

Angela still remembered Aaron's face flush with anger after he had released her from the strong grip. He had been angry enough to punch Kathleen in the face, and stopped just short of doing exactly that before he stormed out the door, slamming it loudly as he exited.

A few days later, two policemen had sat in the living room while he gathered his possessions and hauled them out to a friend's waiting pick-up truck. One cop, apparently a friend of

Jacob's—Angela had yet to verify the rumor—had grinned at Aaron knowingly as he had departed, warning him, "I don't want to see you around here anymore. And, if I hear about a single threat, you'll be hearing from me. And it won't be pretty."

Aaron had had a few run-ins with the law in the past that Angela was beginning to learn about.

She felt her eyes growing weary and was just about to close them when she realized she was sexually aroused and was moaning softly. In spite of herself, she let the pleasurable sensation between her legs continue for a moment before realizing what was happening. *Is someone touching me? It feels like it. What's going on here?*

She suddenly bolted upright in her bed and screamed, a shrill, sharp, short burst. She quickly turned the bedside light on, jumped out of bed, yelling, "Whoever you are, get out of my house."

The room was silent. Embarrassed about the wet spot between her legs, she walked into the bathroom, dried it with some toilet paper and splashed some cold water on her face. She towel-dried her smooth, pale white skin, opened the door and peered into the living room. She listened, afraid to reenter her bedroom.

Silence.

She was terrified.

Abruptly she heard a faint rustling sound coming from the living room. She flicked the hall light on, slowly walking toward the sound. *Should I go in there? I don't feel good about this.*

Her breathing became heavier, more labored, as she tip-toed down the hall. The air was thick and the vibe felt dark.

Don't go in there. She reached the small, moonlit room, flicked a light switch and it brightened. Looking around, she thought everything was as it should be. She sat in the armchair and listened, grabbing a comforter from the couch and pulling it over her sheer yellow nightgown as she noticed small goose bumps creeping up her arm. *Go to bed. No, stay here. Where's my camera? Why didn't I bring it?*

She sat for a few minutes, trying to regain her composure. She shivered with fear, in spite of the warm comforter wrapping her slender body. Finally she stood up. That's when she felt the force, seemingly out of nowhere, cold, thick, powerful fingers grabbing her throat, and slamming her into the living room wall. She heard a crash as she struggled to free herself and knew it was the pastoral picture of a sunlit field her grandfather had left to her in his will. The glass shattered as her head slammed into it and she felt a sharp pain as a shard of glass imbedded itself in the back of her head, blood trickling down the wall.

She flailed her arms helplessly as the powerful hands choked the life out of her. Her vision blurred, her breath came in short, intermittent gasps. She tried to scream but couldn't. She could barely breathe. She couldn't see anyone in front of her but the powerful force of the tightening fingers served as a deadly reminder that if she didn't do something—and soon—she would no longer understand what it was like to be among the living.

She frantically sucked for air but the death-grip only tightened in response. *I'm going to die. Killed by a fucking ghost.* Her thoughts became distant. Then they weren't there at all. She felt her eyes bulging in their sockets, the heat of her face reddening, turning a purplish color as the last semblance of life was sucked out of her. The room darkened, her world grew black.

Suddenly, the front door flew open and Jacob burst into the room. "Let her the fuck go," he yelled at whom he did not know. He watched as the grip released Angela and she slumped to the floor, her body crumpling into an unnatural position as her head bounced off the coffee table.

He hurried to her side, bent down and straightened her body, spreading it out on the throw-rug in the middle of the room. A small cut on her purple forehead dripped blood down her nose and into her eyes. He felt for a pulse. There was none. He had no idea what he was doing—had only seen it in the movies—but he tilted her head up, plugged her nose, put his lips to hers, something he had often thought about doing but never in a situation like this, and began breathing into her lungs.

He stopped, removed his lips and coughed. He looked into her face. Her eyes bulged but there was no movement. "C'mon, c'mon, Angela, come back! Don't leave me!"

He connected his lips to hers and resumed. In his mind, he counted the breaths he exhaled into her lungs. When he got to ten, he felt something, maybe her hot breath breathing into his lungs.

He stopped, propped her head up. She suddenly coughed and spit, loads of sticky saliva mixed with yellowish bits of food dripping down her chin, onto her nightgown. He slid her against the wall, propped her into a seated position as she coughed a few more times and finally inhaled deeply and gasped out a few long breaths before the color slowly started to return to her face.

Slowly her eyes registered her surroundings and she saw the face of Jacob staring into them worriedly. "Are you okay?" he asked.

It took a moment or two before the fog completely lifted. Finally, she half smiled. "You saved my life." She was about to pull him close, kiss him on the lips, but she noticed her chin and mouth were coated with a sticky mixture of goo, that was fast becoming red with the blood that was now dripping down her nose and into her mouth.

"Can ... can you get me a towel?" she asked.

"Sure," he said, realizing he was now sitting there watching her bleed all over him. He was so happy to see her alive, he had frozen to the spot. He walked into the bathroom, grabbed a couple of small bath towels which he soaked in warm water and returned.

"Are you okay?" he asked again as he knelt down and began tenderly wiping the blood, saliva and food mixture off her face. "I mean, can you move, or did you break something?"

Angela slowly began moving her extremities and realized she couldn't feel any pain in them. Except for the small goose egg that was growing on her forehead and the back of her head where the glass had embedded itself. And her throat throbbed dully from the pain of the death-grip. That was going to leave a mark. "I think I'm okay. But, the back of my head." She turned her head, exposing blood-matted hair, lines of blood streaming down the back of her neck.

"Shit," Jacob said. "Let me have a look at that." He leaned closer and noticed a small glass sword, about the width of a pencil, protruding out by a fraction of an inch. He winced. "That doesn't look too good. I think we should call an ambulance."

"No," Angela insisted. "I don't want that. Please, there's a pair of tweezers in the bathroom. Pull it out for me, will you?"

He wasn't in a mood to argue with her. He had returned to her house in a panic about an hour after he had arrived home and his head had cleared. During the paranormal investigation, many nasty and dark thoughts had invaded his mind, thoughts he never could have, never would have on his own. He had become convinced the dark presence in the house had invaded his mind, filling him with an evil rage he had never before encountered. He had thought of murdering her and mutilating her body, had even thought about possible hiding places for it.

And that was only one of the thoughts. He had also thought about brutally beating and raping her, had visions of her helpless struggles as he forcefully and violently had his way with her. Once he had started thinking about it he realized the team hadn't followed protocol. They usually met after an investigation to discuss their thoughts and conclusions before departing for the evening.

He also realized they hadn't had any serious discussions about the nightmarish happenings at the King's Playhouse either. And somehow he felt they were all interconnected but he didn't know how.

But what he did know was Angela should not be sleeping alone in her house tonight. What had tipped the scales was when he had called her cell phone, which he knew she kept in her bedroom and also used as an alarm clock, and a gruff male voice had answered, telling him bluntly, "She's not in," before hanging up. He had quickly grabbed his jacket, ran from his apartment and sped over to her house in his silver Ford Explorer.

He felt the evil presence slowly returning to his mind. *Kill her now. Bury the body in the crawl space below. Do it now.*

He fought to control the dark thoughts. "Okay," he said, walking into the bathroom, returning a few seconds later with the tweezers. He clamped them on the protruding glass, pulled a few times but the small tweezers wouldn't grab. He tried wiping the wound gently with a warm, wet towel but he still couldn't pull the shard of glass out.

"Do you have any pliers?" he asked, admiring her erect nipples protruding from the sheer nightgown.

"There's a tool box in the kitchen," she said. "Under the sink."

He returned with the pliers, wiped the shard clean again, pressed on it lightly and slowly pulled. It moved, ever so slightly.

"Ouch."

"Are you okay?" He stopped pulling, wondering how long the glass was and how far it was imbedded in her head. He still didn't feel comfortable playing surgeon with a pair of pliers. *Push it into her head. Kill her.*

"Sorry, go ahead. Just get it out," she said.

He closed the pliers, snugging them on the glass but trying not to apply too much pressure, for fear of shattering it. He pulled slowly, felt it move slightly, then slid it out in a swift, smooth motion.

"Got it," he said, showing her a half-inch piece of glass, stained red. His rational self hoped it hadn't gone in deep enough to cause any serious damage. And he sighed when he realized there wasn't anything that resembled brain matter dangling on the end of it.

"You're good," she said, smiling.

He picked up another wet face cloth and cleaned the wound at the back of her head. He went into the bathroom and returned with some topical antibiotic ointment and bandages, applying them to both head wounds.

"What do I owe you, doctor?" she asked, as he finished with the small cut on her forehead.

"The doctor would like for you to spend the night at his apartment," he said. "I don't think—no I know—you're not safe here."

A few minutes later, after Angela had cleaned herself up, grabbed a few things and Jacob had cleaned up the broken glass, they stood in the doorway, about to leave. As he opened the door, Jacob hoped the dark thoughts of murder and rape would leave his troubled mind.

CHAPTER TWELVE

"My mind is troubled," Bill Blythe told Ben Ratchet at 7:30 pm on Friday, March 1st.

Ratchet, his tattooed, muscle-bound cellmate, who had spent the last week or so with Blythe, was hardly surprised at the statement. He had watched the old man go from religious proselytizing one minute to confused and dumbfounded mutterings the next. They shared a holding cell in an RCMP detachment on the outskirts of Charlottetown, both awaiting appearances in front of a judge.

Ratchet had been charged with four counts of assault causing bodily harm. He had been in and out of prison since he was a teenager. He'd been convicted of everything from theft, break and enter, attempted murder and many assaults. Not that he necessarily liked assaulting people—although he had to admit as hobbies went, it wasn't the worst one a person could have—he just had an extremely short fuse when it came to people messing with him.

And he used the term messing with him very loosely. Depending on his moods, if someone looked at him the wrong way, it was considered messing with him. The latest battery of assault charges had stemmed from a comment a young kid had made to him outside of Myron's Cabaret in the downtown core of the historic little city of Charlottetown.

Ratchet had stepped out of the bar and stood on Kent Street, having a smoke. Four boys in their twenties, about twenty years his junior, were standing nearby smoking a joint. One of them started laughing, glancing over at Ratchet as he did.

"Are you laughing at me?" he had asked irritably. He was already pissed off because the Plenty of Fish date he had met at the bar had unceremoniously dumped him for another, much younger guy. He had planned on exacting his revenge on that little fool a little later in the evening.

The young blonde kid had looked at him cautiously (Ratchet's grizzled appearance, particularly the thick red beard, costume earrings and clean-shaven head would give anybody pause to reflect before challenging the big man), saying, "No, of course not."

There had been a moment's tense silence before they had all started laughing again. Except for Ratchet. And that was all it had taken for him to fly into a rage and beat all three of them into a pulp. Poor kids had been too drunk and stoned to mount any kind of offense and much too wasted to try and escape, although one had staggered away after three or four powerful shots to his face.

The rage still boiling over in him, Ratchet had walked back into the bar, grabbed the kid who was dancing with his one-time date, dragging him by his long hair out to the street, where he had kicked him repeatedly in the face, head, stomach, chest, anywhere he could find.

He had heard later three of the four kids had ended up in the hospital and only one was lucky enough to be treated with a broken nose and released the same day.

"Are you messing with me?" he asked Blythe, balling his fists and examining the cuts on his knuckles, battle scars from his last altercations.

"No, I'm not messing with you at all," Blythe said.

"You better not be," Ratchet snarled. "Did I tell you what happened to the last guys who messed with me?"

"Yes, you did," Blythe said, walking over from his standing position at the cell bars and plopping himself down on the lower bunk, lowering his gaze so as not to further offend the big man.

Blythe's demeanor suddenly changed and Reverend James Maling lifted his head and regarded the beast in front of him. He had to get out of here. He had people to save, particularly Elizabeth Pelletier. During the week, he had tried a few tacks to sway Ratchet to his camp but so far had not been able to get through to him. The preaching just wasn't working. He thought if he could just get his hands on the big ape, he would be able to impart his religious influence. He had remembered how successful he had been at the church the other day, watching the people's eyes glaze over after he had touched them, smiling as they had exited the building chanting prayers, calling themselves chosen, setting out to save others.

But, he had been unwilling to touch Ratchet, for fear it would result in a severe beating, which he did not particularly need at this juncture in his reincarnated existence. But now, he was seriously considering the idea. A couple shots to the head perhaps, and that would be it. *As long as he doesn't kill me.*

"I think you need a hug," he said to Ratchet.

"A what?"

"A hug."

"Fuck I do. Try it, old man, and I'll smash your head into those iron bars so hard you won't know your ass from your face. Come to think of it, I think I'll do it anyway." He walked over, picked up Maling and slammed his head into the metal cage, their mutual prison.

Maling grabbed Ratchet's head as he was slammed, clamping both ears, focusing with all his evil energy to convert him. He saw a puzzled look go through Ratchet's eyes just as a big fist slammed into his right eye.

Stupefied, Ratchet dropped Maling to the floor. He crumpled to the concrete, grabbed his right eye with his hand, realizing there was a rather nasty cut just above the eyelid that was beginning to flow blood down his face, into his mouth, and down his black and red checkered flannel work shirt.

He wiped away some of the blood on his shirt sleeve, peered up at Ratchet, almost expecting another blow, and asked, "Have you been saved?"

"Yes, I have," he said. "I've been chosen."

"Good, then let's get out of here. I'm going to call the guard, yelling you're beating on me. When he opens the door, rush him. We're leaving."

Maling curled up on the floor and Ratchet began kicking him, careful not to exert too much force on his new mentor. A pool of blood began fanning out around Maling's head and the scene looked suitably convincing.

A rookie cop heard the screams, came running to the cell and immediately opened the door, disobeying RCMP protocol. Ratchet grabbed the young cop, slammed him into the wall, and lifted his handgun from the holster. "We're going," he said. "And, if you know what's good for you, you won't say a fucking word." He leveled the gun at the frightened cop's nose, then for good measure stuck the barrel in his mouth for a moment.

Maling handcuffed the rookie cop to the bed after Ratchet let him drop to the floor.

They both ran down the long hallway, but they could already hear more footsteps in front of them.

"Let me outta' here," one of the prisoners said to them on their way past. "Hey, get me outta' here."

They ignored him as two cops jumped out in the corridor, both leveling their pieces. Maling was walking behind Ratchet, using the big man as a shield. "Shoot them," he said.

Ratchet leveled the piece.

"Drop the gun, stop and put your hands in the air," Detective Redmond said.

Ratchet fired two shots and both cops dove into a nearby hallway, as the bullets whistled past them, chewing into an exit door.

Just before the hallway opened up into a foyer, there was a small interrogating room, just off to the left, the door ajar.

"The room on the left," Maling said. "Slip in there and we can shoot our way out."

They ran the thirty or so feet down the hallway, slipping into the room just as Redmond and the other cop reappeared. Ratchet fired another shot just as they reached the room and the cops ducked as another bullet ricocheted off a wall and sliced into a foyer desk, splintering the wood as it penetrated.

Inside the interrogation room, Maling pointed to a steel chair that was bolted to the floor. Ratchet tucked the piece away, ripped the chair free, turned and crashed through the door from whence they came.

A cop stood in front of it. The door flew open with such force it slammed him into the hall corridor and he melted down the wall, knocked unconscious from the blow.

Detective Redmond backed up firing as Ratchet charged forward, using the metal chair as a shield and shooting. Two bullets pinged off the shield, ricocheting down the hall.

A bullet whistled past Redmond's head and he scrambled to the floor. In the melee that ensued, Maling ran around in front of Ratchet, reached the exit door and disappeared into the night.

Ratchet, slowed by the gunfight, wasn't as quick. As he opened the door, only a few seconds behind Maling, he took a bullet to the leg. He staggered and fell forward, pushing the door closed with his metal shield.

He swiveled around and threw the chair at Redmond, who by this time was in a sniper position on the floor, firing. The chair struck him flush on the top of the head and he fired another shot as he felt his vision blurring.

Ratchet pointed and pressed the trigger of his weapon. Click, click. He had run out of bullets. He limped toward Redmond, arching his good leg for a good kick to the head.

Redmond saw something coming at him in the fog and swept his arm out in a swift, perfectly timed motion that connected with Ratchet's injured leg and brought him down.

Ratchet could see the detective reaching for his weapon as he was falling and turned his body, landing squarely on Redmond, knocking the wind out of him, and kicking away the gun. It slid across the floor, hit the wall.

Redmond heard a crunching sound and winced as he realized a few of his ribs were broken. He struggled to try and free himself, at the same time reaching for his handgun, which he noticed was nowhere to be found. He gasped for breath as he was repeatedly punched in the head. He couldn't get the big man off him. He managed to roll over finally, tasting his own blood that was now pouring out of his facial wounds. He reached up in a last panicked attempt and felt Ratchet's face. He quickly moved his fingers to the criminal's eyes and dug in both of his thumbs.

"You fucking little pig cocksucker," Ratchet said, flinching in pain.

Redmond dug his thumbs in deeper, felt and heard a popping sound as Ratchet's right eye burst out of its socket and dangled by a thread. He screamed in pain, cupped his hand to the dangling eye, just long enough for Redmond to roll out, scramble to the wall and retrieve his gun.

Just as he turned, he saw Ratchet charging at him, his face twisted in a rage he had rarely seen the likes of in his twenty years as a police detective. He pointed the gun and with blurry and blood-soaked vision fired two shots into Ratchet's chest.

Ratchet fell hard on top of Redmond and he grimaced as he heard the cracking sound of more ribs breaking. *At least I'm alive and he's dead,* Redmond thought, as he lost consciousness and light turned to dark.

CHAPTER THIRTEEN

"If you could think of every twisted, nasty thing you could do to a woman I would say yes, I already thought of that," Mark said.

"I had some pretty dark thoughts about Angela," Jacob said.

The team, sans Mister N, sat in Kathleen's apartment at 9:30 pm on March 2nd. They were discussing their experiences at Angela's house during the recent paranormal investigation.

Kathleen had explained the evil presence that seemed to cut right through her body and sat and listened as Mark and Jacob relayed the psychotic, perverted and murderous thoughts that had entered their minds while they were in the house and then just as quickly had vanished after they had left.

"Never mind killing you, I had already thought of where to hide your bodies," Jacob said, turning to the women.

"Me too," Mark said shamefully.

Kathleen shuddered, listening to the stories.

Angela, who had temporarily moved in with Jacob since the terrifying incident, shifted on the couch uncomfortably while her face turned a jaundiced color.

Kathleen suspected there was a lot more to the stories than the guys were telling. She had an image of being tortured by Mark, and then slashed to pieces with a large machete, like the unfortunate victim of some underground snuff porn film. She fought to force the image from her mind. They had assembled to go through some of the data collected at Angela's house and, time permitting, had also planned on reviewing some King's Playhouse recordings and photos. She was anxious to change the subject and get started. She still felt uneasy and had recently visited her doctor, who had doubled her Zoloft dosage. He had also given her a referral for a specialized anxiety clinic. She had faxed the form through and was waiting to hear back from the clinic.

She had been told specialists would be analyzing her physical symptoms, including strapping on a device for a day that would track her heart rate and other vital signs to help doctors determine if physiological irregularities were causing the anxiety attacks.

She felt her heart rate quicken as Mark turned on the digital tape recorder that had been left in Angela's bedroom for part of the night. They were looking for EVPs, Electronic Voice Phenomenon, voices undetectable to human ears but detectable by the sensitive recording equipment.

Mark and Jacob had decided they would not watch the audio-video of Angela trying to sleep. The idea felt creepy to both of them, particularly after she had said she felt like someone had been touching her. Kathleen and Angela would review it together, perhaps in another room later that evening.

The tape started and they sat and listened. They initially heard the sound of water running, a door opening and closing, but Angela explained they were the sounds of her preparing for bed. The tape grew quiet for a few minutes and the team listened intently.

Suddenly a gruff, aggravated male voice: "Why did you leave me, you bitch? Do you think you can get away with this? I'm going to be watching you. You better not get another boyfriend. I fucking hate you. I hate what you did to me."

There was a long pause in the tape as they exchanged nervous glances and Angela's eyes widened. Kathleen moved closer to her, putting an arm over her shoulder.

The voice started again: "You think you're so clever. Your friends must be stupid to hang around with you. You're so selfish ... shut up ... I said shut up."

Another long pause. "Turn it off," Angela said.

Mark clicked it off.

"If you don't want to listen to it, we can do this another time," Kathleen said, hugging her friend.

Another pause. Angela blinked and rubbed her eyes as a tear rolled down her cheek.

"Let me get you some tissue," Kathleen said, getting up, going into the bathroom and returning a few seconds later with a whole roll of toilet paper. She peeled off a length, wiped Angela's face and handed her the toilet paper.

"That sounds like my ex-husband. He used to say shit like that to me and then apologize, saying it was only coming out because he felt like I didn't love him as much as he claimed to love me," Angela said. "But, I want to get this over with. Turn the tape on."

Mark turned it on and the voice started up immediately: "You use people for sex ... You don't love anybody but yourself ... What do you see in me?"

They twisted uncomfortably in their seats: "You use your friends ... you don't love me ... you won't miss me ... you're not affectionate ..."

A long pause and it continued, "I want you back baby ... please come back ... please, please, please ... come back to me. Things will be great. Why the fuck did you do this to me? I'm going to fucking kill you, you little bitch."

They heard a painful scream, followed by wracking sobs and the tape went silent. Angela wiped tears from her eyes as they listened some more. A few minutes later, they heard the sounds of the struggle connected to the blue bruises scarring Angela's neck, but the only voices they heard were Jacob's and Angela's

"Wow," Kathleen said, after the tape was turned off. "That was freaky. We've never captured that many EVPs before."

"Did you see anything at all?" Mark asked. "Or do you want to do this another time?"

"No, I'll be okay," Angela said. "It just brings back some pain. I didn't see anything. I heard something in the living room, I went in there and that's when I was attacked."

She pointed to the marks on her neck, which the team had already noticed by now.

A few hours later, after they had gone through the still images and parts of the audio-video recordings collected in the living room and bathroom, and finding nothing except a repeat of the creepy voices that were on the audio recorder, Angela and Kathleen stood up to go into Kathleen's office and watch the video of Angela sleeping, or trying to.

"What's this?" Jacob suddenly asked, pointing to a white image on a digital picture someone had snapped in Angela's bedroom. It showed a large white ball near the window. If you used your imagination, you could almost make out the hooded image of a man. "It looks like an apparition."

While interpretations of photographic evidence differ widely among paranormal investigators, there are those who claim no one has ever photographed a conclusive image of a ghost. Many orbs, or mysterious balls of light, can be explained by dust reflecting off light. They studied the image.

"I think it's dust reflecting off moonlight," Kathleen said, pointing to a small beam of light that appeared to be shining through the window. She had seen her fair share of images and ghost videos on YouTube, and was convinced almost all of them were fakes. And, of course, there was also pareidolia, the psychological phenomenon whereby a vague image or stimulus is seen as significant, or something other than it really is. In other words, people see what they expect or want to see, like faces in clouds or a face in the moon. Or, they hear what they want to hear, like strange messages when records are played backwards or strange voices in the night.

"It's definitely inconclusive," Mark said, as the women walked down the hall and he pulled out the data of the King's Playhouse.

A few minutes later, while Mark and Jacob listened to a digital recorder, Angela and Kathleen returned and sat down. Mark turned off the tape.

"I think Angela and I will watch the rest of her bedroom video tomorrow night," Kathleen said. "Angela would rather listen to this stuff with you guys right now. But she's got some clothes, money and some other things which we need to get from her house first." Since the attempted murder-by-strangulation a few days ago, Angela had been too frightened to return to her home.

"I'll come with you," Mark said.

"Me too," Jacob said.

Kathleen thought about how their expressions had darkened the last time they were there and didn't care for the idea much. "No, I think it's better if I go alone. I don't like what happens to you guys in that house. And Angela, for obvious reasons, doesn't want to return right now, not even during the day."

Mark started to protest, but Kathleen was already walking toward the door with her jacket. She picked up Mark's truck keys on her way out. "You guys stay here. I won't be long. I'll bring some pizza back. None of us have to work tomorrow. I'm taking Black Death."

"You got your cell?" Mark asked, as she opened the door to leave. She nodded, smiled nervously and closed the door behind her.

She looked up into the sky as she walked down the moonlit street, noticing how the weather had already started to become milder. Birds were returning, trees were starting to bud, grass was greening up, and the first signs of spring were in the air. She made a mental note to try and get to Poverty Beach one day soon, one of her favorite places to go and be mesmerized by the ocean waves and infinite view out to sea. *I could use a chill-out day at the beach.*

She was startled to see a police cruiser roll down the street slowly, the cop driver eyeballing her as he passed.

She fired up Black Death, pulled out and began the short drive to Angela's house on Hillcrest Avenue. She made a mental note to go to the library soon do a historical search on Angela's home. Apparently Angela's grandfather had owned it for 50 of his 86 years and, as far as Angela had known, there were at least two owners prior. One had been a married couple with three children who were for all intents and purposes, normal. *But who knew, really, until you actually started digging around.* But somehow Kathleen was convinced the incident had nothing to do with the house's history but had everything to do with the evil spirits they'd stirred up at The King's Playhouse.

Her phone rang just as she parked in front of the property. "Hello."

"Kathleen?"

"Yes."

"This is Detective Redmond. Listen, I'm sorry to bother you at this hour, but there is something I thought you should know."

"Yes, what is it?"

"You remember Bill Blythe?"

"Yeah."

"Well he escaped from the holding cell last night. You haven't seen him, have you?"

"No."

"Well, you make sure and call me if you do, okay?"

"Sure."

There was a moment's pause. "I know this sounds crazy," Redmond said, "but I'm beginning to give your theory of possession some consideration. Bill Blythe did not look like Bill Blythe when he got away yesterday. I don't know how else to say this, but he looked like someone else."

Kathleen didn't know what to say so she said nothing.

"The other thing," Redmond said. "He might be a little pissed off at you and Mark, maybe he'll come after you. You guys be careful."

"Okay." Kathleen wanted to end the conversation. She was getting nervous, especially sitting outside her friend's house. "Is that it?"

"Almost. Maybe I've asked you this, but I need to ask you again. Did you guys see anything during your King's Playhouse investigation?"

"We heard screams, saw a bloodied and battered apparition of a woman."

"Did she say anything to you?"

"Yes, she did. She told us to beware the chosen one, for he is evil."

"Do you have any theories about that?"

"We're still working on it. We haven't gone through all the data yet."

"Do you mind if I call you sometime, maybe talk about what exactly you saw there?"

"No," Kathleen said. "Not at all."

"Okay, and if you come up with any more theories, please call me, okay?"

"Will do," Kathleen said. She clicked the call dead. *Shit. Bill Blythe on the loose. Or James Maling on the loose? There's something he's not telling me.*

She grabbed the flashlight from the glove box, took a deep breath, got out of the truck and walked up the cement path to the front door. She turned the key slowly, looking around, expecting Maling to be coming after her. *He will come after me though. I know that. Don't ask me how I know but I know.*

She heard something creak as she opened the door and stepped in the hallway, and then noticed the wind had suddenly picked up, the branches on the tall mature trees lining the historic street beginning to sway to and fro with its force. *It's just the wind, keep going.*

She flicked on the hall light, shone the flashlight beam into the living room, trying to determine if anything was obviously amiss. From a distance, everything looked to be in its place. She shone the light at every nook and cranny to see if everything was normal. Nothing looked out of place. *Everything in its place and a place for everything.*

She reached into the coat closet, grabbed a large duffle bag, and walked into the living room, shining the flashlight to a wall switch that she flicked on, illuminating the room. She went into Angela's bedroom and methodically began picking through an assortment of clothes she had been instructed to retrieve. She went to the bed, lifted the mattress, removed a small purse from underneath, shoving it in the duffle bag alongside the clothing. She shivered. The room had suddenly gotten cold.

I'm almost finished. Don't think, just keep going.

The front door suddenly slammed shut with a loud bang. Kathleen jumped, letting out a frightened scream, and dropped the duffle bag, some of the contents spilling out. *Take the offensive.*

She approached the front door with the flashlight. "Whoever you are, get out of this house," she said, when she reached the hallway. "You're not wanted here."

She felt it again. The same dark and terrifying force passed right through her and she shuddered, trying to contain the negativity she felt would spew forth from her mouth any second. She felt her heart thumping in her chest but continued her monologue. "I said get the fuck out of here. You're not wanted!" She finally reached the front door, her entire body trembling with fear. She grabbed the door handle, swung it closed to the sound of the whistling wind, which by now had intensified. *Possibly a strong nor'easter coming at us.*

She slowly walked back into the bedroom, taking deep breaths, trying to slow her speeding heart. *Hang on, kid. You can do it.*

She opened the bedroom door and her eyes widened in shock at the sight in front of her. The items she had put in the duffle bag were strewn all over the bed, the dresser, and the floor. A pink lace bra even hung from the bedside lamp. What horrified her were the words, scrawled on the eggshell-colored wall above the queen-sized wooden bedpost, written in a black greasy substance. The words were hand-scrawled with large fingers and there were a few smudged hand prints below the dire warning: *THEY'RE COMING!*

"Oh no. Oh my God, no!"

In a panic, Kathleen rushed around the room, collecting the clothing, trying hard not to forget anything even though her first impulse had been to flee the house, screaming and yelling. After a few minutes, she examined the room. Satisfied she had everything, she reached in her pocket for the flashlight, slung the duffle bag over her shoulder and left, being careful to turn all the lights off and lock the door.

She pressed down hard on the steering wheel, trying to stop her hands from shaking as she navigated the truck, first to pick up two large pizzas and then to drive back to her apartment. Thankfully, Black Death performed admirably on the trip home. She knew only too well he could get temperamental at times. As she exited the truck and walked to her apartment, she shielded her eyes from the blowing wind, which was now picking up dust and small bits of debris and firing them at her.

Entering the apartment, she was greeted by three wide-eyed people, sitting and staring at her, their expressions somber.

Mark stood up, immediately noticing her chalkiness.

She set the pizzas on the coffee table.

"They're coming," she said, running into his arms, hugging him.

"Who's coming?" Jacob asked, reaching for a slice. He had by now repositioned himself on the couch beside Angela. The two sat almost touching.

Kathleen went over her experience, her expression becoming more animated and talking quicker as she neared the end of the ordeal. Finally, she said, "I don't know who, but they're coming. What should we do?"

"What can we do?" Mark asked, sitting down with her on the small loveseat across from Angela and Jacob.

Jacob went into the kitchen, returning with four plates. He served up pizza slices to them.

She explained the other part of the story, that Bill Blythe had escaped from the holding cell, how she felt there was more to the story, and that Detective Redmond would be contacting them with some questions in the future. "We could always call him," she said. "Tell him what happened at Angela's house, at the theatre. This is just getting too much for me."

Her hands began to shake some more. Mark cupped her hands and gently squeezed. His touch warmed and comforted her.

They only stared at her in silence for a few minutes, munching on pizza. Finally, she asked, "What's with all the somber looks? What did you guys find on the recordings?"

"We heard Elizabeth, if that's who she is," Mark explained. "And we heard a lot of other screams, shouting, talking, a cacophony of eerie sounds."

"That's a big word for you," Jacob observed.

Mark ignored the comment, continued, "It's almost like our visit unleashed a flurry of paranormal activity that somehow has gotten way out of control."

"It seems more like a fury of paranormal activity," Angela said, adjusting her leg slightly so it touched Jacob's knee. He didn't seem to mind. "The question is how do we stop it?"

They sat silent, trying to figure out the conundrum.

To Kathleen's mind, Elizabeth held the key to unlocking the paranormal nightmare. She had warned them about the chosen one, and perhaps she wanted to help them. After all, she hadn't exactly harmed them. Kathleen also wondered about some of the more traditional methods. During their investigations they had learned four ways to get rid of bad spirits.

One, say a prayer in the haunted house around a white candle, a symbol of love, asking the spirits to leave.

Two, have a priest bless the house and its inhabitants.

Three, have a clairvoyant contact the spirits, ask them to leave, then infuse the house with a positive energy to replace the vacant negative energy.

Four, go in and freak out at the spirits, yelling and screaming for them to leave.

Although they had implemented some of the methods with some degree of success in the past, right now none of them seemed to make any sense. They were not religious, although maybe it was time they started believing in God. They had to believe in something good, now more than ever.

Although they had never used mediums during their investigations, believing their use to be unscientific, they had called them in after a few investigations to help clients expel evil spirits. In some cases, it seemed to have worked. But, for whatever reason, Kathleen did not believe a medium would help in this case.

And she doubted trying to freak the spirits out would do any good. She felt this tidal wave of dark energy that had been unleashed was much too powerful to be swayed by a group of people yelling at them, mediums, even men of the cloth.

Her thoughts finally turned to Elizabeth. *That's it. We have to contact her.* She had watched many paranormal television shows where someone would actually contact a spirit and channel the energy and personality of the spirit through his or her body. But she had never believed any of those stories. The only time they had ever had a conversation with a ghost was during their encounter with the apparition of the murdered Elizabeth Pelletier. And she wasn't even sure that qualified as a conversation. The woman had merely repeated something twice, apparently at Kathleen's urging.

"I think we should try and contact Elizabeth Pelletier," Kathleen said, standing up and walking into her office. She returned a minute later with a laptop, sat down next to Mark, and started typing.

"What are you doing?" Mark asked.

"I'm checking PEIPI's inbox."

"Uh-oh," she suddenly said, the chalky expression revisiting her features.

"What?" Mark and Jacob asked in unison.

Typically, PEIPI would be lucky to get one request per month for a paranormal investigation.

"We have twelve new contact requests for investigations," Kathleen said. "Oh, sorry, thirteen. Another one just came in now."

CHAPTER FOURTEEN

That same evening, Reverend James Maling crouched behind a storage shed in the backyard of Bill Blythe's home. He had unfinished business, and he waited for the police officer inside to go for a coffee, or get called out on a more important matter. He didn't think it would be too long now.

He had just walked into the home of a neighbor a few doors down, plucked a large carving knife from the kitchen counter knife rack, sauntered into the living room, where a fat drunken slob was burping, drinking beer and channel-surfing, and quietly sliced open his throat.

He had smiled when the man's eyes widened in disbelief as a large gash appeared on his neck, blood gushing out, spraying the bowl of chips perched on his lap.

He knew Rodney Chambers' wife would be home any minute, only to find her husband slumped over in a pool of blood, the television blaring, the half-finished beer bottle still clutched in his hand. And he expected a shriek that should be enough to rouse the cop guarding Thelma.

He wiped the carving knife with serrated edges on his pants and enjoyed how it glistened from the glow of the small porch light. He had helped himself to a few of Rodney's clothes before leaving, a heavy jacket and a red baseball cap, which he was thankful for now as the wind picked up and blew some debris in his face and he ducked back inside the comfort of the small metal shed.

Rodney's not going to miss these now. Not in his condition.

He certainly wasn't a candidate for saving, Maling knew that much. Too many bad habits and a mouth so foul it needed a rather good cleansing with a good bar of soap. And Maling didn't even think that would work with the likes of Rodney Chambers. *No. That man was the seed of the Devil.*

Like clockwork, Maling heard a door close, a few seconds later a loud shrieking scream. He saw a uniformed police officer exit the Blythe house, dash over to the Chambers' residence and bang on the door only for a split second before entering.

Good, Maling thought. *The cop is gone. Close by, but gone. I should have time.*

He quickly fired up the gas-powered chainsaw that was hanging up right beside him, keeping him company.

"Put that down," Bill Blythe said.

"To hell with you," Maling responded, running the six or so steps up the back porch, disappointed at his language. "Go away. I have work to do here."

He had an answer for the locked back door. He buzzed through the wood surrounding the deadbolt and pushed it open. Thelma was just lifting her bulk from her favorite lounge chair by the time he made it to the living room. *This is too easy.*

She looked at him in total shock. "Have you gone crazy?"

"I haven't taken leave of my senses, Sweet-Cakes. I've come to them."

He brought the chainsaw buzzing down at her head and she instinctively raised an arm in defense. The chainsaw cut through her wrist and her hand fell on the carpet, blood spewing from the amputated limb.

She only got to the beginning of what could have been a loud and annoying scream before Maling raised the chainsaw again and decapitated her. Her bloodied head bounced on the carpet twice before rolling underneath the small metal television stand. Her headless body even managed to take two or three steps before barreling forward and crashing on top of the television, shattering the antiquated picture tube and creating a mini fireworks display—pop-pop-pop.

Maling glanced down at the headless body that had rolled onto the floor draining blood and twitching. He smiled, admiring his handiwork. *That'll teach you to be so self-indulgent.*

He heard sirens as he dropped the chainsaw, walked out the back door, down the well-worn path to the end of the yard, through a missing board in the fence, and disappeared into the night.

CHAPTER FIFTEEN

On Saturday afternoon, March 3rd, Nick Calibri, aka Mister N, sat in a wooden chair at his kitchen table wondering if he should call Mark Riley one more time. He had called five minutes ago and left a voice message that Mark had not returned. He wanted to tell him he no longer wanted to be a paranormal investigator. And he didn't want to say it over the phone, fearing Mark would take it the wrong way and it might affect their friendship.

Truth be told, Mister N had been having a lot of paranoid thoughts lately and he no longer felt mentally fit enough to navigate the sometimes stormy seas of the paranormal. Of course, he wouldn't say that to Mark. He would merely tell him his fifteen-year-old son Henry was giving him problems again. Mark had heard that before and would understand. You see, Henry had learned how to manipulate his father, becoming a master of the infamous guilt trip.

Mister N had divorced his wife Mena thirteen years ago after a short one-year marriage. Mena had sought and won the better part of the custody battle. Mister N only got to see Henry on the weekends, hardly enough time to be a good role model. As Henry grew up and Mister N got older, he had started feeling guilty about not being there for his son, even though Mena had drifted from one abusive relationship to the next and was hardly a stabilizing force in the boy's life.

Mister N had become so consumed with guilt that Henry would say "jump" and his dad would ask, "How high?"

Every time his phone rang, he ran to it in a panic, thinking that Henry, who had begun acting out and behaving badly, had gotten himself into trouble again and needed his dad's help. He was so worried the next call would be a cry for help from the troubled teen he never turned his cell phone off. He slept with it right beside his ear every night.

The all-consuming guilt began manifesting itself in other disturbing ways. At times, Mister N would think people were out to get him and he often woke up in the morning fretting about any number of things that occupied his dysfunctional mind.

A few months ago, he was in the middle of a renovation (he was a handyman) with a handful of other contractors and Henry had called, crying on the phone because some bully had punched him in the face at school. Mister N had flown into a rage, cursing and swearing, throwing his tools around and had finally stormed from the jobsite, the contractors dropping their jaws wide-eyed, regarding him warily as he had left. He had received a call from the property owner later that afternoon asking him to come and pick up his tools and his paycheck. His services were no longer required.

He was afraid to travel far for fear Henry would need him. He wanted to stay close at hand, be at his son's beck and call 24/7. In many ways, the meaning of his life came down to ensuring Henry was all right. Outside of that focal point, he found very little satisfaction in anything.

If Henry, or some of his other friends (there were only about four) didn't call him for an extended duration, he would begin to fear the worst. In a very short time one little thought would escalate into a full-blown panic and paranoia attack.

He had very little interest in the opposite sex. His ugly divorce had left him irreparably scarred. He viewed relationships through a negative lens, believing any long-term intimate involvement with women eventually led to heartache and emotional ruin. Rather than long-term commitment, he preferred short-term carnal satisfaction from the opposite sex. He was not a good person to ask for relationship advice.

He rubbed his hands together now, looking at the clock. *It's been fifteen minutes. I wonder if Mark's okay. Maybe something happened to him?*

He felt his stomach begin to knot, stood up, walked to the fridge, pulled out a plain slice of white bread and poured himself a glass of milk. He sat down chewing on the bread and drained the milk, hoping it would settle his stomach. It didn't.

What the fuck happened to him! Call me, Mark! Are you okay?

A few minutes later his mind was bursting with negative thoughts. And not only about Mark. About the whole team. And about his son. He stood up, breathing deeply, something a psychiatrist had once told him would help. *Take a walk. It'll do you good.*

He looked out the window, seeing sparrows erratically circling the large oak trees in the backyard of his small rented house. The sudden high winds and snow squalls of last night had given way to clear, sunny skies this morning and he doubted he would even have to shovel his walk. The snow would probably be completely melted in an hour or so if he just let the sun's rays do the work.

He grabbed a light jacket (it was pleasantly above freezing) and left his house, walking the two or so blocks before he reached Main Street. He had to admit, the fresh air made him feel a little better, but not a lot.

He approached an elderly man on a street corner, matted hair, wrinkled grey suit, proselytizing and waving some religious pamphlets around. "You need saving," the man said, handing him a flyer.

You're right. I do. Should I take it? Mister N had a love-hate relationship with religion, as he had been inundated with it since early childhood. On one hand, he wanted something or someone to believe in, and on the other hand he had grown tired of his siblings constantly telling him to pray to God and all his problems would be solved. Sometimes he felt his beliefs bordered on atheism and at other times, when the negative thoughts became overwhelming, he found himself crouched down beside his bed praying for inner peace, something he often thought he would never be able to attain.

He grabbed the flyer and walked past the man, listening to him rant. "Read it and be saved. Come to our meeting at the church next week," the man said, his voice trailing off as Mister N picked up his gait, putting distance between them. He crunched the flyer into a ball and put it in his pocket without reading it.

He was surprised to see a young woman preaching and handing out flyers on the very next street corner. *What's happening to this town?* She looked to be in her mid-thirties, about five years Mister N's junior, with large black-rimmed nerdy-looking glasses, curly black hair, and large white teeth.

Her body was average, her breasts enormous. They jutted straight out from her beige jacket, announcing themselves in fine fashion.

At least that was Mister N's opinion. *I wonder if she'll like me. Not a bad rack. Would she go for a prematurely greying guy with nice brown eyes? Lots of people tell me I'm good looking.*

"Would you like to be saved?" the woman asked, approaching with a flyer, her pupils dilated.

Mister N took the flyer and feigned interest. "I might," he said.

"Good," she said, interpreting it as affirmative. "We're having a special ceremony next Sunday at the Holy Trinity Church in Georgetown. Would you like to come?"

"I might," Mister N said, extending his hand. "I'm Nick."

"Mary Contrelli," she said, offering a horse-toothed smile. "Would you like to talk about God with me?"

"Right now?"

"Sure, we can go to Tim Hortons or somewhere more private if you'd like," she said, winking, adjusting her posture, and pushing her voluptuous breasts in his face to make a point.

Mister N probably would have declined if it weren't for those huge melons hovering a few inches from him. They seemed to defy gravity. "I live close by. You can come to my house."

She looped her arm around his with a smile and they trotted down the street. A few minutes later she sat at his kitchen table drinking coffee, talking about how amazing it felt to be a chosen one. She had taken her jacket off and a tight white t-shirt accentuated her ample bosom; her best feature in Mister N's humble opinion.

"I just feel reborn," she said. "A completely new person with a new appreciation for life."

"That's good," Mister N said, trying hard to focus on her face as she spoke.

"I used to worry all the time, get paranoid about things, but all that's gone away."

Mister N had to admit it would be nice not to worry so much. *Why hasn't Mark called? What's Henry doing?* "How did you so suddenly get reborn?" he asked.

"Reverend James Maling converted me from my wayward ways. Would you like to meet him?"

"I guess I can do that next Sunday."

"Oh I wouldn't wait until then. I can have him come over now if you'd like." Before Mister N, who had heard nothing of PEIPI's theories on Maling, could answer, Mary pulled out her cell phone and speed-dialed a number.

"Reverend," she said. "I have another recruit for you. 136 MacLaren Avenue."

"Wait a minute here," Mister N said. "I don't know if I want this ... not now anyway."

She stood up and smothered his face with her ample breasts, wrapped her arms around his head and smiled.

Mister N was about to protest but he was enjoying himself too much.

"When he's gone we can have some fun," she said.

He couldn't say anything if he wanted to. He could barely breathe.

CHAPTER SIXTEEN

"I don't know where he is. I called him back and he didn't answer. Weird," Mark said to Kathleen as she sat at the kitchen table early that evening reading *The Guardian*, one of the local papers. He had just returned from hauling some debris, but left his phone in Black Death and missed Mister N's call earlier that day. He had planned on taking the day off, but in the end got the impression that Kathleen needed some private time to herself. She was that kind of person and he had come to understand that about her.

"That is weird for him," Kathleen agreed, returning her attention to *The Guardian*.

She had gone out earlier in the day to run some errands and been disturbed by the number of bible thumpers she encountered on the street. She counted six in a six-block radius and had mentioned it to Mark as soon as he arrived at her apartment.

She now had nineteen contact requests for paranormal investigations and responded to all of them with one simple keystroke strike and a form letter thanking them for their request and telling them PEIPI would be in touch with them at its earliest convenience. Thank God Jacob was a website designer. It made PEIPI's job a lot easier.

Angela and Jacob had left her apartment late last night and they agreed to reconvene this evening at Kathleen's in order to try and contact Elizabeth.

"Did you see this?" she asked Mark, her face suddenly turning ashen white.

"What?" Mark asked, slipping his coveralls off and approaching.

She showed him the headline: *Two Islanders Brutally Murdered.*

Mark frowned and sat down at the table.

"Thelma and her neighbor were brutally murdered," she said. "It says here police are not yet releasing details of how they were killed, other than to say it was brutal. And they're looking for Bill Blythe for questioning in connection with the murders."

"Shit," Mark said. "Do you think he'll come after us?"

"We were responsible for him getting charged."

"That's true. What do you want to do?"

"Maybe we should call Detective Redmond?"

"For what? Police protection?"

"I don't know, but it's probably time we explained our theories to him."

"Okay, go for it."

Kathleen picked up her phone and was about to dial Redmond, when it suddenly rang. "It's Jacob," she said, glancing at the call display.

"Have you heard?" Jacob asked, referring to *The Guardian* story. They also discussed the bible thumpers and sudden barrage of paranormal contact requests.

"I was just about to call Redmond," Kathleen said. "Are you guys still coming over?"

Jacob explained that Angela felt out of sorts from last night and they had decided to hunker down for the evening. They would not be coming over to Kathleen's.

"Do you want me to call you if Redmond comes over tonight? He may want to talk to you. And he might want to know about Angela's house."

"Go ahead and tell him if you want," Jacob said, after a short pause during which he discussed it with Angela. "And yeah, call us if he comes over. Maybe talking to a detective will make Angela feel a little better. She thinks this stuff has gotten way out of hand for us to try to handle on our own."

Kathleen hung up and immediately speed-dialed Redmond. She got his voice mail and left a message.

She felt the edge returning and struggled to control her thoughts. *We're fucked. No, no, no, we're not. Calm yourself girl. This isn't the end of the world.*

Mark saw her eyes go distant and touched her hand. She smiled weakly.

"Are you sure you're up to contacting this Elizabeth?" he asked.

"Do we have a choice?"

Mark didn't answer and Kathleen knew it meant acquiescence. "I think I'm going to rest for a while," she said, kissing him, standing up, and going into the bedroom.

"I'll be here if you need me," he said, grabbing a beer from the fridge, popping the can open and settling on the couch with the television remote control. He took a swig, turned the television on, and began channel-surfing.

In bed, Kathleen twisted and turned, trying to find a comfortable position. Finally she settled, lying on her stomach, her head tilted away from the window. The moonlight shone through, dimly illuminating the room. *Elizabeth? Are you there? We need your help. Speak to me. Please!*

Silence, except for the muffled voices of the television in the living room. The voices weren't loud enough for her to understand but she took comfort in the sound, knowing it meant Mark was close by if she needed him.

She had thought of popping another Zoloft before going to bed to keep the anxious thoughts at bay, but then remembered she had already taken twice the recommended dosage today. She would have to will her mind to take a different direction as she knew only too well that a panic attack would render her completely helpless in the face of danger. And yet she couldn't shake the feeling danger was very near—and very real.

And her work situation had been getting more stressful. Last week, she found out Linda Wellington had applied for, and been accepted for, a transfer. She had been replaced by a twenty-year-old female assistant who held down two jobs, drank two buckets of coffee a day, and bounced off the walls. She was pleasant enough, that was, when she wasn't texting someone while speaking. In between her job duties or during them—it didn't matter to Susan Debility—she had her smartphone going incessantly, either sending or receiving texts, checking Facebook, playing games or surfing the internet. Ron Baglund had already told her twice to put it away and she didn't seem to care or want to heed the warnings.

Kathleen knew it was only a matter of time before he threw one of his temper tantrums again. Susan seemed intent on provoking him with the phone.

The situation at work only added to Kathleen's already very high stress level. Next week, she decided, she would talk to the vice-principal and at least let him know of the developments regarding the onset of anxiety attacks. *Don't think of that word. Not now anyway.*

She tried to blank her mind and focus on napping, hoping it would refresh her mentally. She started counting backwards in her mind, an exercise she often did to fall asleep. Some people counted sheep, Kathleen just counted. *100, 99, 98, 97, 96, 95 ...*

Mark heard a knock at the door. He got up to answer it. *Who the hell is that?* He looked through the tiny peep hole, and saw the image of his friend Mister N. Not trusting his eyes, he asked, "Who is it?"

"Mark, it's me," Mister N said from the other side of the door. "Can I come in?"

He had been worried about Mister N earlier. He quickly opened both locks, and swung the door open. "Hi," he said, as Mister N walked into the living room, a glazed look in his eyes.

"Kathleen's not feeling well, so I don't think you should stay long."

"No problem," Mister N said, sitting on the couch. "Can we talk about God?"

"What?"

66, 65, 64, 63, 62, 61, 60 ...

The bedroom window shattered before Kathleen had a chance to register what had happened. She had just started to doze, thought she was dreaming. But the voice that accompanied the loud noise informed her in no uncertain terms this was not a dream.

Maling had just crashed through her bedroom window.

"There you are," Maling said, blood dripping from a small cut on his head. He wielded a machete and began swinging it wildly while coming toward her. "You don't need to be saved," he said. "You need to be killed."

Kathleen rolled across the bed just as the machete came down hard, slicing into the blankets and missing her by inches.

One sharp knife, she thought, lifting a pillow to defend herself. *As if this is going to work.*

Swinging the machete, Maling charged. It sliced through the pillow and a shower of feathers flew in the air, slowly drifting to the floor as he continued attacking.

Kathleen dropped the pillow, picked up a bedside lamp, yanking the cord out of the wall and started swinging it around. "Help me," she screamed, as Maling advanced, cutting off her path to the door and cornering her in the room. "Mark, help me."

The machete connected with the lamp shade, sliced through it, breaking the light bulb with a pop.

Kathleen crouched down in the corner with the lamp as the machete struck it. She winced as the blade connected with the back of her hand, slicing a large gash open and spraying blood. *Is this what it feels like to die? Not like this. Please, not like this.*

Mark heard the commotion and ran down the hall. He pulled open the door and saw Maling standing over Kathleen, grunting as he swung the machete, destroying the bedside lamp. It wouldn't be long before his efforts would knock it out of her bloodied hands.

Mister N sat on the couch, the corners of his lips pointed upward, staring blankly at the television. *Why am I here again?*

"Over here, you fucker," Mark said, throwing a book that he had picked up from the bedside table. The book connected with the back of Maling's head, distracted the preacher for a split second. That's all Mark needed. He tackled the man and they landed on the floor, twisting and turning as they grappled. Mark grabbed the machete handle, trying to wrestle it from the evil entity. *Holy fuck is he strong for an old bastard.*

Kathleen ran into the living room in desperate search of her phone. Just as she arrived, her apartment door burst open and Redmond sprang into the room, gun drawn. "Where is he?"

She pointed down the hall with a trembling hand.

By the time Redmond reached the bedroom, Maling had pinned Mark to the floor and was sitting on top of him with the machete raised over his head. Both of Mark's arms were cut and bleeding profusely.

"Drop the weapon," Redmond shouted.

Maling didn't turn around. He didn't give a rat's ass about the body of Bill Blythe, although he would never use that terminology to describe his sentiments. He brought the machete down.

Redmond fired two shots. Loud popping sounds echoed in the small room. Both bullets penetrated the back of Blythe's head, and splattered the panicked face of Mark with gray matter and blood.

Mark instinctively moved his head and the machete came down, digging into the hardwood floor, Bill Blythe's body slumping over it.

By this time, Kathleen was back in the bedroom, a bloodied towel wrapped around her left hand.

Mark pushed the body off him, crawled out from underneath, gasping for breath.

Mister N walked into the room, bent down, and touched the shoulder of the lifeless form that was once Bill Blythe. "He's dead," he said, his eyes electrifying with an energy he never before had possessed. Slowly a satisfied smile emerged on his face.

"It's over," Redmond said. "This nightmare is over."

CHAPTER SEVENTEEN

A few days later, Kathleen sat on her living room couch surfing the internet on her laptop computer, thinking her nightmare was far from over. And *the* nightmare was far from over.

Immediately after her near-death experience she had a panic attack, collapsing on the floor and freezing into a catatonic state. She vaguely remembered Redmond and Mark carrying her into the living room and gently placing her on the couch, while the apartment filled with police, forensic experts, and paramedics. She distantly heard the voice of Redmond questioning Mark and Mister N.

One voice rose above all the others. It was the voice of Elizabeth Pelletier telling her to go to church to find the answer. Tomorrow was Sunday and there was a special gathering of people who had recently been born again and were about to become indoctrinated into their new Christian faith.

Kathleen had come out of her anxiety attack just in time to be taken by ambulance, along with Mark, to the hospital. He had received 68 stitches to gashes on his forearms and she had received thirteen stitches to the cut on the back of her left hand.

Dr. Heeling had arrived at the hospital, looking concerned. A few days later he had tripled the dosage of Zoloft on her prescription.

On Sunday she had called work, requesting a leave of absence, explaining she was traumatized by the vicious attack on her life. The vice-principal had responded understandingly, encouraging her to take as much time as she needed before returning. She conveniently omitted the anxiety attacks on the phone but knew it was only a matter of time before she would have to tell him about them.

The next day, she and Mark had gone down to the police station and been interviewed by Detective Redmond for two hours. She had explained everything to him. He had nodded intently, no longer questioning the believability of her story.

As a result of her information, he had also interviewed Angela and Jacob and investigated Angela's house. He even stayed there a few nights and reported to the team he had not noticed anything unusual. So Angela had, at least for the time being, moved back into the property. But she decided to sell it and a Coldwell Banker *For Sale* sign now stood on the front lawn.

Mister N had also been interviewed and Kathleen had phoned Detective Redmond for an opinion. Redmond had said, "He seems fine to me. And his story checks out."

Kathleen wasn't so sure about that. He had been acting strange lately. She had called him a couple of times just to try and get a read on his mental state. Both times the calls had gone to voicemail and he had not responded to her messages. *Highly unusual.*

They had not been able to do any further paranormal investigations or go through any more data after what had happened. But one woman, who called herself Martha Pelletier, had been persistently calling and emailing, telling Kathleen, "It's extremely urgent you investigate our property. It will shed some light on what's been happening and what's going to happen in Montague and Georgetown."

Kathleen wasn't in a mindset to deal with the call at all, fearing another investigation would lead to another, and perhaps a more debilitating anxiety attack. So she had downloaded a subscription smartphone app that allowed her to block the woman's number, at least until she was mentally ready to deal with it. Who knew when that might be?

She had spent the first three nights after the attack at Mark's small rented house just around the corner from her place, but started missing the comfort of her own digs and returned home. Typically, Mark was the one who stayed at her apartment, not the other way around.

The study of the paranormal takes a person in many different directions and Kathleen was curious about the term psychometry as it popped up on her computer screen. She had brushed passed Mister N on the way to the hospital, accidentally touching his hand and jumping back as a dark energy permeated her body. Although Wikipedia defines psychometry as "a form of extra-sensory perception characterized by the claimed ability to make relevant associations from an object of unknown history by making physical contact with that object," Kathleen wondered if the associations could extend to people. She remembered listening to a clairvoyant on television who explained the term more broadly, describing it as a vibe a person has, either when they walk into a room or meet another person. The woman went on to explain that sometimes the vibe is much stronger with physical contact, like that of a handshake. And, she had said, everyone has it, to greater or lesser degrees.

Kathleen digested the information with a shudder as she clicked the window closed, returning to the inbox of her email account. Three new paranormal investigation requests stared at her ominously, bringing the total to 44. They were coming in fast and furious. She grimaced, put her laptop on the coffee table, and closed the window. She could feel a dull pain in her head. It was time to take another pill.

Her smartphone started vibrating across the kitchen counter as she swallowed the pill and she picked it up. Since her last attack, she had switched it to vibrate mode as the ringing sound would often startle her. She saw Mark's number and smiled, knowing he would be over soon.

"Hi, honey," she said, trying to compose herself. He was cognizant of her slow mental collapse and lately hadn't said anything about his plan of buying a house for them. She wondered if he had changed his mind. She didn't think she could blame him if he had. *Who wants to be with an emotional wreck?*

"Baby, could you come and get me? I'm at the Johnson house in Georgetown."

"Sure," she said, feeling a bit drowsy from the pill. "What happened to your truck?"

"Black Death's been stolen."

CHAPTER EIGHTEEN

Earl Sotterton was a good man who believed in justice. The flipside of that was he despised injustice. A hardworking fisherman he had drowned in a fishing boat off the coast of Prince Edward Island on October 3rd, 1851, during a storm referred to as *The Yankee Gale,* perhaps the fiercest storm ever to wreak its deadly path of destruction on PEI. According to reports, over 100 people died in the two-day storm and over 100 vessels, most of them American fishing boats, sank as a result of its powerful fury.

Earl had worked hard his entire life and died at thirty-six. His body had been found at sea and buried under what was now The King's Playhouse Theatre. But now the ghost of the man walked the streets, unleashed during the PEIPI paranormal investigation.

And he wasn't in a very good mood. He wanted vengeance for the death of his sixteen-year-old son, who had been stabbed to death at the hands of Micky De-yodeler, the great, great grandfather of Joleen De-yodeler. He had been following Mark around with interest, mainly staying put in the extended cab of Black Death with his mouth shut, until he had recently overheard a conversation with Detective Redmond, reminding Mark to come in and file a police report on the woman who had attacked him with a butcher knife. Reading Mark's thoughts, he had understood only too well the evil this woman was capable of. He knew she had screwed over a lot of people, including the unfortunate landlord, Nigel Pearson.

He tapped Black Death's dashboard as he rolled down Highway 4. He loved the name and thought it the perfect vehicle to serve justice upon De-Yodeler. "Let's get this bitch," he said, smiling as the motor suddenly roared louder, as if in response.

He slowed and turned right on Highway 316, which would eventually take him to Iona Road, where he had heard she still occupied the premises illegally. He checked the time: 7:36 pm, turned up AC/DC's *Highway to Hell* and grinned as he navigated Black Death down the highway.

I like this new music. I hope she's around when I get there.

A few minutes later he arrived in front of the rural acreage, pulled over onto the shoulder of the road. A few motorists had gawked at him as he sped out of Georgetown after stealing the truck, although he liked to think of it as borrowing it to take out the trash. He knew their wide-eyed expressions were less related to the way he looked (he stood about six feet tall with short grey hair and handsome, chiseled features) than they were related to the way he didn't look. He hadn't made his apparition visible. To them, Black Death was driving driverless.

He turned the volume down, killed the engine, turned the lights off, and eyed the property. *Good. Her truck's there and the lights are on. She's home.*

Earl waited patiently for a few minutes and saw a dark figure move to the front bay window, peer out, and then disappear. There was a tree-line bordering the property that almost completely blocked the house from highway traffic and he doubted she could see Black Death from where she stood, a good hundred feet away from where he was parked.

A few minutes later Joleen appeared outside, walking toward the barn, probably to feed or kill one of her ducks.

Earl took the cue, fired up Black Death, locked up the four-wheel drive, put pedal to metal and barreled down the small dirt driveway.

She was halfway to the barn and her eyes widened at the oncoming vehicle. She made a run for the barn. It was a little too late as Black Death clipped her leg, spun her up in the air, onto the hood where she bounced a couple of times before rolling off.

Earl slammed Black Death into reverse, peeled back about twenty feet, spinning out tufts of grass and dirt, and slammed it into drive, hoping he wasn't being too hard on the transmission.

He rumbled forward, but she rolled and Black Death missed its mark. He was a little slow turning around for another approach and he noticed her slowly get up, her left leg bleeding and twisted in an odd position. Blood dripped into her eyes from a cut on her forehead.

She yelled something incomprehensible to Earl but he couldn't help notice her eyes widen in fear as she realized Black Death had no driver—at least no visible driver. He went for his second approach, but by that time Joleen had limped onto the back porch and slipped inside the back door of the house.

Not knowing what else to do, Earl waited.

A minute later she returned with a double-barrel shotgun, stood in the doorway and fired off a blast of buckshot. The little steel pellets penetrated the windshield and it shattered.

She began reloading and Earl roared Black Death around to the front of the house.

He parked on the front lawn, facing the bay window.

A few seconds later she reappeared, this time crouched down in front of the bay window. She popped a window open and pointed the weapon at Black Death. She wasn't expecting what would happen next.

Earl put the truck in reverse, backed up thirty or so feet, turning, narrowly missing another round of buckshot. He stopped, slammed the truck into drive, and floored it. Joleen was reloading when she saw it. She looked up in shock, stepping back, dropping the gun in her panic, as Black Death crashed right through the window, slammed into her, and pinned her up against the wall separating the living room from the kitchen.

She cried out in agony as she heard her bones breaking, felt her pelvis snap, and knew she would probably never be able to walk again for the rest of her life.

"What do you want?" she asked, over the noise of the tires losing traction and spinning on the hardwood floor. Blue smoke and the stench of burning rubber began to fill the room.

"I want you dead," Earl said.

"Why?" she asked, blood dripping from her open mouth.

"Die Yodeler," he shouted, backing up a short distance. He slammed it into drive, was about to floor it again, then suddenly stepped on the brake. *May as well enjoy this a little while.* He watched her overweight bulk slowly begin to slump over. He wanted to time it perfectly.

When he thought her head had slumped to bumper level, he released the break and hit the gas, slowly at first and, as the tires found traction, accelerated, slamming Black Death into Die-Yodeler, crushing her skull, plastering her body into the wall. Debris rained down on the hood of the truck from the severely damaged wall as the tires lost traction, began spinning, and burning rubber. Earl turned the ignition off and stepped out, regarding the bloodied, crushed corpse.

"Why? You asked me why?" He didn't care that she could no longer hear him. "Because you're a waste of space, that's why."

"And Micky De-Yodeler murdered my son. That's also why. I hope you burn in hell."

CHAPTER NINETEEN

Kathleen sat with Mark in the Holy Trinity Church in Georgetown Sunday morning, wondering why Mister N stood up at the podium, with a woman beside him whom she did not recognize. Reverend Jeremy Bourne had emerged, said a few short words, and then introduced Mister N whom he had referred to as our "profound new guest speaker."

The small church was full and a few people even stood at the back. She recognized the man in the wrinkled grey suit, sitting a few rows across from her. A few people looked wide-eyed at Mister N as he approached the podium. A few more people stared at Kathleen. She had become somewhat infamous after news broke of Blythe's attack on her life and subsequent killing by Detective Blaine Redmond.

Kathleen had tried unsuccessfully to contact Elizabeth last night but had convinced Mark to attend the service with her, telling him something wasn't right regarding all the bible thumpers that were running around town. He hadn't felt confident about her mental state but finally agreed.

Mark had immediately reported Black Death as stolen yesterday, and had received a phone call late last night from Detective Redmond who said the truck had been found at the small rural property he had attempted to remove debris from previously. It had been discovered with a mangled corpse attached to it: the body of Joleen De-Yodeler. The vehicle had been towed to a police facility where they were combing over it for evidence.

Mark's alibi had checked out, and he had immediately reported the vehicle stolen. That gave Redmond no reason to suspect him. But Redmond had told him it could be a while before the vehicle would be returned.

Mister N cleared his throat at the podium as Mary sat down in a chair behind him, beside Reverend Bourne. "I'm glad to see so many people in attendance here today," he said. "Today we're going to talk about a view of the Christian faith that may not be familiar to some of you."

Kathleen wondered where he was going with his sermon as the conversational drone of the congregation slowly subsided and they focused their attention on the speaker. She noticed an upside down cross dangling from his neck and didn't know what to make of it. It evaporated from her mind as he continued speaking.

Mister N cleared his throat. "Today we're going to talk about how God has let us down."

A quiet murmur rolled through the church.

"That's right," Mister N continued, gesturing with both hands outstretched, "He's let us down."

Reverend Bourne frowned but let the profound guest speaker continue.

"You tell me," Mister N said, griping the microphone with both hands. "What kind of God would allow famine, escalating murder rates, wars, natural disasters, destruction of our planet, to name just a few?"

He paused for effect. "Well, I'll tell you what kind of God allows that: a spineless, weak, coward of a God."

There was some murmuring in the audience and Kathleen was about to get up and give him a piece of her mind. She was spiritual but did not attach her spirituality to any particular religious denomination. She had probably been to church a half a dozen times in her adult life, although as a child she had attended more often than that.

Mark grabbed her arm as she stood. "Wait," he whispered. "Let's see where he's going with this."

She sat down, noticing a few expressions were dazed, subservient, a few others disapproving. *What the hell's going on here?*

"Well, I've been chosen to tell you this is a time for change, a time for a new wave of religious faith to enter your consciousness. It is time for a new God. And that God is Satan."

More murmuring in the audience. And then something else. A humming sound, coming from some of the congregants: "Mmmmmmmmmmmmmmmmm   ... Mmmmmmmmmmmmmmmm."

Reverend Bourne stood up and walked briskly toward Mister N, who simply turned and pointed a finger at the preacher, who quickly retreated to his seat.

"It's our turn!" It was the voice of Elizabeth Pelletier, inside of Kathleen's head. *"Put a stop to this. Now!"* Without realizing it, she had brushed aside Mark's hand on her leg, jumped up from her seat and marched purposefully to the front of the church.

"What you say is blasphemous," she said, turning to the congregation. "What's with you people? You shouldn't stand for this lunatic talk from him. Reverend James Maling, murderer of Elizabeth Pelletier: You're not a man of the cloth. You're a Satanist. Expel him from the church."

"You have sealed your fate in the bowels of hell," Mister N snarled.

Bourne ran toward Mister N, attempting to grab his arm. Mister N merely stepped aside and the reverend crashed into the podium, tipping it over. It rolled off the three-foot stage, splintering into pieces as it crash landed.

Mister N pointed at Bourne and he backed up with his hands in front of him as a shield from the powerful evil force.

Mark got up and rushed to Kathleen's side. He could see her starting to tremble as a few starry-eyed congregants rose and walked toward her. By the time he had reached her, the man with the matted hair and wrinkled suit, unknown to both of them, had taken hold of her arm and was trying to pull her up to the stage, close to Mister N.

"Let go of her," Mark said, grabbing the man's arm.

Then it started. Fire broke out. Flames rose first from the church organ, then the front doors were ablaze and soon flames were licking all around them.

"You will pay for your insolence," Mister N said, raising his hands as the flames snaked up the wall behind him. "You will burn in hell."

There was mass pandemonium as the fire spread quickly. Kathleen started coughing and felt different hands tugging at her. "Mark, where are you?"

"I'm here," he said, "I have your arm."

"Yeah, well so do about three other people."

Amid coughing, yelling, and screaming, he pulled her toward a side rear exit. "Over here." He managed to free her from the other hands and arms that were her pulling in another direction.

There was a crowd of people screaming and yelling when they arrived.

"It's locked," someone yelled.

"We're all going to die in here," another panicked voice said.

"We'll burn to death," a woman's frantic voice said.

"Burn in hell ... burn in hell ... burn in hell," Mister N said, over the panicked screams, coughs, and voices.

"Move over," Mark said, pushing his way through the crowd, Kathleen in tow. They arrived at the door and both started kicking it. The smoke was thick and burned their lungs, the heat intense. They dripped with sweat.

Kathleen heard some blood curdling screams, could smell burning flesh. She knew people were dying. She only hoped she wouldn't be one of them as she counted to three, charged into the door, and heard a crunch. "Something's breaking, Mark. Hit it again."

He backed up a few feet and ran toward the door, crashing into it hard. It flung open and he stopped just before falling over. "Let's go."

Kathleen glanced back for a second just in time to see Mister N (only it wasn't really him anymore, was it?) striding along the stage, engulfed in flames, the flicker of an evil grin illuminating his face. She leaped through the doorway just as the ceiling caved in and a fire ball of debris came crashing down beside her, crushing and igniting five panicked people rushing to escape from the inferno.

They ran along a corridor, which circled the small building, and opened into a reception room equipped with a kitchen. A few small classrooms and some bathrooms also adjoined the corridor, which eventually led to a back door, a concrete porch and twenty or so steps leading down into a rear parking lot. Thick black smoke began enveloping the area and their progress slowed. She could barely see Mark in front of her. Flames licked up the walls, threatening to penetrate the thin drywall any second and send them to a fiery grave.

A shrieking woman, flames swirling up both legs, ran past Kathleen. Kathleen instinctively pulled her small jacket off, tackled her, and started patting out the flames as screaming people hurried past. A few of them stepped on the woman's head, chest, and legs. Mark heard the woman's agonized cries, pulled off his jacket, and began smothering the flames. They extinguished the fire but Kathleen could see and smell burning flesh. Some of the woman's polyester pants were stuck to her scorched skin and she continued screaming. Kathleen was kicked in the head by someone escaping the inferno. She fell off the woman, rolling in the hallway, her hands covering her face. Mark quickly grabbed her and pulled her tight to the wall to avoid getting trampled to death.

There was a momentary pause in the rushing foot traffic. "Stay against the wall," Mark said, as he knelt down and helped the woman to her feet. He grabbed her left arm, Kathleen instinctively took the right and they labored down the corridor, helping the woman along.

There was a crash and some screams behind them and Kathleen glanced back as a massive ball of flames and debris rained down from the ceiling, crushing and burning more unfortunate victims.

Whoever was still in the hallway behind them was now trapped by a wall of flames and would probably not get out alive.

Kathleen had one hand outstretched now, feeling her way. She could no longer see six inches in front of her face and her skin was burning up from the intense heat. Fire burned all around them, and people shrieked and screamed. The historic building crumbled.

"We're going to make it," Mark said between coughs. They could hear sirens now and knew they were getting close.

"Around that corner," Kathleen said.

"What corner? I can't see anything."

"I'm going by feel," Kathleen said. "I can feel cold air over there. The door must be open."

She took the lead, running her hand along the wall, feeling for what she had envisioned to be a left turn toward an exit. It was more of a gut feeling and if she had to explain it she wouldn't be able to. One time she had met a woman in a Charlottetown coffee shop and during their twenty-minute conversation asked her if she lived in the north.

Surprised, the woman had asked, "How did you know?"

"I don't know," Kathleen had said. "I just knew."

Similar things had happened too many times for Kathleen to ever consider it a coincidence. She just knew better. Usually, when her phone rang she knew who it was before looking at the call display and long before picking it up. It was just a sixth sense, or psychic power she didn't know. But she knew she had it, whatever you wanted to call it.

"Ouch," she said, running her hand through a flame that had engulfed part of the wall.

"Are you okay?" Mark asked.

The woman's screams had ebbed into a soft moan as they trudged along and the shrieks of the dead and dying grew distant.

"Yeah," Kathleen said. "Hit a hot spot. We're getting close."

Suddenly she felt the corner to her left. "This way. Straight ahead, about thirty feet."

"We have to run," Mark said. "Look."

She glanced back and saw the hallway engulfed by a huge fireball. With a whooshing sound, it rapidly raced toward them.

"Can you run?" Kathleen asked the woman, her lungs burning.

"I'll try."

"You go first," Mark said. "I'll be right behind you."

Kathleen got behind the woman, pushing her forward, Mark behind her, pushing her forward.

They reached a corner and saw daylight through the thick smoke, just to the left. The woman collapsed as she reached the outside concrete porch and Kathleen fell on top of her just as she heard a large chunk of the ceiling collapse behind her.

It was mayhem outside. Paramedics were helping the wounded into waiting ambulances and firefighters stood by dousing the flames. Kathleen coughed, spit up a black ball of mucous, and wiped her watery eyes. She couldn't see anything and realized her eyebrows and eyelashes had been singed.

"Mark, Mark," she said blindly, still wiping her eyes. No response. "Mark," she yelled. Nothing. Finally, through watery eyes, her vision came into focus. And she saw Mark, rolling around on the lawn below in flames.

Instantly two firefighters rushed over and sprayed him white, extinguishing his burning body.

A firefighter helped her up. "Is there anyone still inside?" he asked.

"Yeah, but I doubt they're alive."

Two paramedics picked up the injured woman and led her over to a waiting ambulance. Kathleen wanted to run to Mark but her lungs were still too depleted from inhaling smoke. It was all she could do to lean against the firefighter who had helped her up.

She saw the woman they had rescued being led by firefighters into a waiting ambulance. The woman stopped near Kathleen. The side of her face was black, red and blistering. She coughed four times and then caught her breath.

"Thank you for saving my life," the woman said. "I'm Martha Pelletier."

Kathleen nodded and the woman was led into an ambulance.

"Let's get you some oxygen young lady," the firefighter said, taking Kathleen's arm.

"Wait," Kathleen said, as she neared Mark, who was being attended to by paramedics. "You okay, honey?" she asked.

He forced a smile that came off more as a wince. "I'm good. Just minor burns."

She noticed the entire back of his shirt had burned through to the skin, the same for both sleeves and most of the back of his jeans. It appeared as if the damage was limited to his backside. The front of his clothes looked intact, although it was hard to be sure, since he was also covered in white powder.

Mark was led away in an ambulance and Kathleen stood outside breathing bottled oxygen, getting examined by paramedics and waving to him as he left.

Still in a haze, she realized just how lucky she was to be alive. For the second time. She wondered how many people had lost their lives in the fire as she watched the Holy Trinity Church burn to the ground, firefighters trying to put it out. They were too late. The fire had already engulfed three quarters of the building and it collapsed around them. They would not be able to save it.

Martha Pelletier. Where do I know that name?

CHAPTER TWENTY

"What about her?" Mark asked, studying Kathleen's face from his bed at the King's County Memorial Hospital in Montague the following evening.

"She's the one who has been calling me so much. Maybe she can shed some light on what's happening around here," Kathleen said.

"What do you want to do?" Mark asked, cringing from the pain of the second-degree burns that covered most of his back and arms, extended down his buttocks, and halfway down his legs.

They were talking about Martha Pelletier. After Kathleen had been released from the hospital yesterday evening, she had remembered the woman and how persistent she had been on the phone, falling just short of insisting the team investigate the paranormal happenings at her house.

"I'd like to talk to her," Kathleen said. "I don't think this is over."

Mark shared a room with another male burn victim who groaned in pain. He looked much worse than Mark, probably third or fourth-degree burns to most of his body, including his face. His life was in serious jeopardy.

Mark had been told he would be released in about a week as long as doctors could ascertain there was no infection as a result of the burns. His total recovery time, however, would be a month or more.

Of the 150 people who had attended the service yesterday, 78 had met a horrible, fiery death and the death toll was still rising. The hospital was overflowing with burn victims of the tragedy and many had been transported to hospitals in Charlottetown. Gossip was abuzz and Kathleen had been getting lot of strange looks lately. Murder and mayhem seemed to follow her wherever she went.

"If you think it would help," Mark said, grimacing in pain. "But your mental state? Are you up for it?"

A nurse entered and opened the privacy curtain separating the two patients. Kathleen caught a brief glimpse of the frightening sight of the other suffering patient. She had no stomach for blood and gore—or burns, for that matter. "Yes I am," she said, unconvincingly.

"Okay, but be careful," he said.

"By the way, thanks for saving my life. I love you Mark," she said, her eyes welling with tears.

"I love you too."

A few minutes later she stood at Martha Pelletier's bedside. Both of her legs were bandaged from the toes to her hips, and the right side of her face was bandaged. Kathleen had learned she had suffered third-degree burns. In her late sixties, Martha was a tall, slim woman with short grey hair and soft features. Martha smiled at the sight of Kathleen. "Thanks for saving my life," she said, after Kathleen had introduced herself and identified the other rescuer as her boyfriend Mark. "And thank Mark for me, please. How's he doing anyway?"

"Looks like second-degree burns. He'll be okay. How are you?"

"I'm in a lot of pain but grateful to be alive."

They exchanged some small talk before Kathleen got to the point. "Maybe this isn't the right time to ask you about this, but you said you could shed some light on what's been happening around here."

"I can," Martha said weakly.

"I'm all ears."

"You know of Elizabeth Pelletier?"

"Yes." Kathleen wasn't sure at first how much to tell this woman but made a snap decision that full disclosure was best. "She warned us about Reverend Maling, her alleged killer. And she's been inside my head a few times."

"That's spirit attachment. She's been at my house a few times and told me about you, how intuitive you are," Martha said. "She was the daughter of my great-grandfather. You read about how she died?"

"Yes."

"How much research have you done on Maling?"

"Very little. There's been so much going on lately."

"I've learned why Maling killed her, why all the haunted happenings have recently been occurring," Martha said.

"Why?"

"Maling killed her because she possessed a secret ... more than one actually."

"Go on," Kathleen said, anxious to hear the mystery solved.

"The first secret Elizabeth learned was that Maling was actually recruiting members into Satanism under the guise of Christianity." She paused for effect.

"That explains a lot of things," Kathleen said, remembering the deaths of Bill Blythe and Nick Calibri. Out of respect for the dead she no longer wanted to think of him as Mister N.

After all, he had his good sides. It wasn't just black and white, as it seldom is.

"The second thing she learned was a way to persuade these followers away from Maling's evil teachings."

"What was that?"

"I know you're going to think this sounds crazy, but there was an ancient sword handed down through my family for generations. I think this sword was used by one of Jesus's followers, to fight religious battles on the side of justice and goodness."

"Where is the sword?"

"I'm getting to that," Martha said, wincing as she tried to adjust a leg that would not obey her command.

"Are you okay?"

"I think so. Anyway, Liz came to me a week or so ago, I can't remember now, telling me about the sword. It possesses the power to send the evil spirits back to the spirit world. You have to touch the ... infected person with the sword for it to work."

"I'm confused," Kathleen said. "Does the sword only work for spirits?"

"No," Martha said. "Liz told me she could touch Maling's followers with it and they would somehow see the light. That's why she was at the church that fateful day when she was brutally murdered. She wanted to get people to her house so she could touch them with it."

Things were beginning to add up. "So that's why Maling wanted her dead. To get the sword and destroy it. Did he ever find it?"

"No, and that's part of the reason he's back. If he finds it, this town is doomed."

"Where is it?"

"It's buried in my basement crawl space. My house used to be Elizabeth Pelletier's. You have to find it and rid this town of the evil taking over. And, please, find it fast. We don't have much time."

CHAPTER TWENTY-ONE

I'm running out of time, Jacob thought, staring at his computer screen the next evening, realizing the upstart author's website he was designing needed to be ready to launch in a few hours. William Blackwell had just completed his second novel, *Nightmare's Edge*, released yesterday and he wanted the link on the new website that would allow people to click it and purchase the book on Amazon. Apparently, Blackwell had done a lot of social media promotion, steering his followers to the new website, yet to be live. He had also told Jacob it was one of his very best creations.

Lucky he's not a high-maintenance client, he thought, as he went to work on the new design.

To a lesser degree, the black cloud had enveloped Jacob earlier in the day and he had gone down for a nap. He didn't mind napping though. He had read somewhere napping makes you smarter. Look at all the Latin American countries with their siestas. Weren't they a lot happier than North Americans, who not only ignored the biological callings of the mid-afternoon blahs, but worked right through them?

He had to admit the force of the black cloud had been weakening; in part because he hadn't given it—*or her*—a lot of thought lately due to the murderous happenings right in his own backyard. Some things were more important than the black cloud.

Oh, he could still feel it lingering, but much less pervasive than only a few short weeks ago. He also had another woman to think about: Angela. The few days she had spent at his home had been very enjoyable and Jacob somehow thought the dynamic of their relationship had changed.

Not that they had done anything, but they had come awfully close. Jacob had slept in his living room, giving up the comfort of his bedroom to Angela. One night, they had decided to stay in, watch movies on the 65-inch plasma television screen. Jacob had noticed Angela squirming on the small couch next to him as he reclined on the futon bed in front of the television. He had finally asked her, quite innocuously, if she would be more comfortable on the futon. He had meant to switch places with her, but after she had smiled and climbed in beside him, he didn't know what to do. And he liked her close to him. So they had watched *The Bourne Supremacy*, a movie they had both seen before but loved.

After a few minutes of talking and joking, Jacob had innocently put his arm around Angela and soon they were cuddling and watching the film. It could have gone farther, but they both didn't let it. And, although it was only cuddling, it seemed their relationship had become closer and more intimate than before.

A part of Jacob still worried that Angela was not safe in her house, although she courageously had maintained she would be okay there. They were also talking more often now, at least twice a day. She had mentioned some potential buyers were scheduled for a second showing, and maybe the house would sell quickly so she could move on to safer and more pleasant digs.

Although some historical analysis had been done, Jacob and the team had yet to discover the identity of the jilted lover spirit who had so terrifyingly occupied the premises earlier. All they knew was that he had disappeared, at least for now.

Jacob worried about Angela's safety often lately and, after learning about the other near-death experiences, also worried about the health and welfare of Mark and Kathleen.

His phone rang. It was Kathleen.

"Are you up for another paranormal investigation?" she asked, after they had exchanged greetings.

"When?" he asked, realizing the solution to the website dilemma that had been nagging at him all day. He would use a stock template now to facilitate the book links and create a custom design later. That way, he could take the required time to come up with something sensational for Blackwell, whom he believed was a very good writer.

"Tonight," Kathleen said, the nervousness in her voice unmistakable. "It's urgent."

CHAPTER TWENTY-TWO

"Where are you going?" Detective Redmond asked Kathleen as she sat in the back seat of Jacob's SUV, about to pull away from the curb. He was beside them in his black, unmarked cruiser, the window rolled down.

I'm going to have to think on my feet. Wait, I'm sitting down. "We're going to Charlottetown to have dinner," she said.

"Where?" he asked.

"The Pilot House," Kathleen said, not wanting to break her promise to Martha Pelletier.

"Anything unusual happening at your house?" he asked, eyeing Angela, who at the last minute had decided to come along.

"Everything's good," she said, forcing a smile. "And thanks so much for your help."

"Not a problem. Listen, I would like to talk to all of you again sometime. I need to make sense of what's happened around here and I know you have some theories."

"Sure," Kathleen said. "I'll call you later in the week and we'll set something up."

"All right, have a good night. And drive carefully. Visibility isn't that good tonight." As he was about to pull away he added, "Oh, one more thing. Do you know what caused the fire at the church?"

"It seemed to spring up spontaneously from a few areas at the same time," Kathleen said. "No idea."

"Oh," the detective said, scratching his goatee. "That's what everyone else is saying? Are you going to Nick's funeral?"

They nodded, waved, and pulled out, Redmond still parked in the middle of the quiet residential street, watching them curiously as they disappeared.

They were actually heading to Martha's Pelletier's rural acreage property, a few miles northwest of Georgetown on Hazelgreen Road. *Maybe I should have just told Redmond,* Kathleen thought. *What am I hiding anyway?* But then she realized it had more to do with keeping her word. She had assured Martha of complete confidentiality and the woman had given her a house key, extending entry permission to PEIPI members only. Kathleen took client confidentiality seriously and knew the permission did not extend to the law.

Martha, a widow, lived alone in the turn-of-the-century home on five acres. Other than a temperamental female black cat named Spike, whom Kathleen had offered to adopt until Martha was released from the hospital, they were told no one else would be there.

Kathleen had briefed the others prior to leaving, so they knew what they would be up against, or at least they'd know what they were looking for. This wouldn't be a typical paranormal investigation, if there were such a thing. Their mission was to go into the basement, find the wooden cross marker indicating where the sword was buried, dig it up, and use it to purge Georgetown and Montague of the deadly evil presence that had invaded these otherwise peaceful and serene locales.

With any luck, although Kathleen was yet to piece together exactly how, they would also be able release the restless spirits back into the spirit world.

Sure, they would have audio and video recording devices with them, but their primary purpose was not to investigate—it was to retrieve and leave.

There was a ubiquitous silence in the SUV as Jacob navigated Highway 3 east and Kathleen supposed they all had their own problems to deal with. They were all inwardly grieving over the loss of Nick and the church fire tragedy, even though they had barely mentioned it. She could just feel the sadness permeate the silver Ford Explorer.

There was also a nervous vibe in the vehicle. Did this emotionally strung-out group of paranormal investigators really think they were any match for the evil forces they were up against? Kathleen supposed they did, but would they hold up? She knew Jacob and Angela still smarted from their heartbreaks of late and hadn't Angela almost been strangled to death by some perverted, jealous, psychotic entity?

And her own psyche was less than normal; that was an understatement. She had noticed the edge always lurking in the back of her mind now. What had also started bothering her were the blank spaces developing in her mind, the result, she guessed, of the medication. At times, she would try to concentrate on a particular task and her mind would go blank, almost as if the medication was dumbing her down, robbing her of an important part of her personality.

Luckily, she had received another call yesterday from the anxiety treatment center in Charlottetown. Dr. Heeling must have pulled some strings because the six-month wait had turned into six days. She would be going in next week for an assessment to determine viable treatment options.

"How are we going to do this?" Jacob asked.

After a short pause, Kathleen said, "Two of us should go into the basement and one person should keep watch at the front door."

"I'll keep watch," Angela offered, not wanting any part of digging in a dark crawl space.

"Sounds good to me," Jacob said. "I'll get the shovels when we arrive."

A few minutes later they pulled into the driveway of the secluded property and Jacob parked in front of the aging house. Martha Pelletier collected a meager pension and it probably wouldn't be long before she would have to sell the property and look at something requiring less maintenance. The house had seen better days.

At a glance, Kathleen could see the wooden siding needed painting, the asphalt shingles were starting to curl, and a few wooden railings were missing from the wraparound deck. Stepping up onto the porch, she also felt the wooden floor creaking under her weight, and the decking starting to sag. Rot had infected it. Either it would need major repairs, or a complete removal and replacement. She doubted Martha had the money for either.

Angela grabbed a duffle bag and Jacob walked toward a small steel storage shed to retrieve some shovels.

"Be careful on this deck," Kathleen said, glancing back at Angela who had begun walking up the rickety stairs. She nodded, tiptoeing to the front door.

Kathleen tried her key. It stuck at first and she jiggled it a few times, glancing around at Jacob approaching with a pick-axe and two shovels. There was a large barn on one corner of the property, its red paint peeling off. The lawn, already starting to green up, was well manicured and there was a patch of dirt partially dug up that evidently Martha had planned on using as a vegetable garden to augment her pension.

Kathleen heard an anxious meow and a hissing sound as she opened the creaking door of the house, shining a flashlight inside. She briefly saw Spike's angry yellow eyes glowing in the moonlit living room and the black cat disappeared, scrambling to wherever her favorite hiding spot might be.

Martha had told her Spike was skittish around unknown visitors. She had stumbled upon Spike hiking through the forest near the home. The cat would disappear whenever she saw her. But over the course of a year, putting food outside, coaxing Spike with bite-sized cat treats, she had finally domesticated what was once a feral animal. However, the long imprinted instincts of mistrust had stayed with Spike. She would not automatically trust most visitors. You had to earn her trust. And once you did she was one of the most affectionate animals you would ever encounter, according to Martha, anyway.

They walked in, set down the duffle bag, fished out 2-way radios, flashlights, and two digital cameras. That's all they would need right now. They didn't plan on hanging around.

"I'll stay in the living room," Angela said, turning an old table lamp on and plopping herself down on a floral-patterned couch. It was positioned beside a large bay window, offering a view of the driveway leading up to the property. "I've got a great view from here."

"Okay," Jacob said. "You got your walkie-talkie?"

"Yeah, right here."

"Here's a flashlight," he said. "You see or hear anything, call right away, okay?"

"No problem," Angela said, offering her most confident smile.

A few minutes later, after doing a walk-through of the property, turning on lights, snapping photos, shining light into unlit crevices and corners, Jacob and Kathleen went into the basement of the home. It had a dirt floor, smelled damp and one small ceiling bulb barely illuminated the eerie crawl space.

They found the small makeshift cross that marked the location of the ancient sword and felt the ground with their hands.

"It's pretty hard," Kathleen said. "Start with the pick-axe, soften it up a bit, then we'll start digging."

Jacob elevated the pick-axe over his shoulder, was about to swing it down and stopped. They both heard a creaking sound. "What's that?" he asked.

They listened, heard it again, accompanied by a whistling noise. "Sounds like the wind has picked up," Kathleen said.

Jacob radioed Angela who confirmed the tree branches had started to sway from the sudden gusts of wind blowing in.

"Roger that," Jacob said into the walkie-talkie. "Over."

He swung the pick-axe into the dirt four or five times and it began to soften. "Did she say how far down this thing is buried?" he asked.

"I forgot to ask," Kathleen said, putting the shovel down, digging out a clump of dirt and throwing it aside. "It's still pretty hard. Maybe a few more minutes and we can start digging."

He beat the ground while Kathleen watched. "If there is anyone in here could you make yourself known to us right now please?" Kathleen asked.

Jacob paused, wiped his sweaty brow, and listened. They waited for a minute, but heard nothing.

"Just thought I'd try," Kathleen said. "Doesn't hurt to ask."

A minute or so later they both worked with shovels, digging at the hard ground.

The walkie-talkie squelched out a hissing sound. "Come in, Jacob, come in. Over."

He put his shovel down and grabbed the two-way radio. "Jacob here, what's up? Over."

"This cat is starting to make a lot of noise, meowing and hissing in the living room. I'm getting scared, over."

"What do you want to do, over?"

"I don't know, over."

"Do you want us to come up or keep digging? Over."

"Keep digging, over."

"Roger that, over and out."

Kathleen suddenly felt a cold chill. *They're coming.* She thought she heard a voice. "Did you hear that?" she asked.

"What?" Jacob asked, resting his arm on the shovel and taking deep breaths. They were down about a foot now and about three feet in diameter.

"That voice." She leaned her shovel against an antiquated oil furnace. They were quiet for a few seconds, listening to the faint whistling sound of the wind punctuated by the frightened meowing of Spike upstairs. The old house creaked occasionally.

"All I hear is the wind and the cat," he said, continuing to dig.

Kathleen picked up her shovel, believing the voice was in her head, and rejoined Jacob. *Is my mind playing tricks on me, or is that you, Liz?*

About twenty minutes later Jacob heard a crunching sound, the steel of his shovel grating on wood. He knelt down, wiping the dirt away. "It's a box."

"Break it," Kathleen said. "The sword must be in there."

Suddenly they froze, staring at each other wide-eyed as a loud crash echoed through the house, followed by screaming. Jacob was the first to leave, grabbing the pick-axe and scrambling up the rickety stairs.

Kathleen was right behind him. They reached the living room and stopped abruptly. The man with the matted hair and wrinkled suit held a gun to Angela's head and was backing out of the house, his arm around her neck. The front door had been smashed open and splintered wood and broken glass littered the hallway. The color had drained from Angela's face as she stared in terror at her friends, mouth agape, eyes bulging.

Jacob stepped toward the attacker, pick-axe raised.

Kathleen stood in the doorway to the cellar, trying to think of a plan. Finally the recognition registered with her swimming thoughts. *That's Milton Blyster. I used to see him in Charlottetown, asking for money, drinking in the streets, and collecting cans and bottles. I thought I knew him.*

"I wouldn't do that if I were you," Milton said. "Unless you want this lassie here to join the afterlife." He tightened his choke hold on her throat and she squeaked.

Jacob stopped.

"What do you want Milton?" Kathleen asked, as he reached the doorway.

There was brief flicker of recognition but it disappeared in an instant. "I want that sword," he said, reaching the doorway and leaning on it, steadying the gun at Angela's temple.

Kathleen could see a beat-up red pick-up truck idling in the driveway. *Funny we didn't hear it come in.* Her voice was tight with emotion. "Okay... I'll go get it. Let her go."

He stepped back in the hallway, and leaned against the wall. "The sword first."

The door suddenly flung open, connecting with Milton's head with a loud thunk. He staggered back, blood dripping into his eyes from the ensuing gash.

Jacob stepped forward, raising the pick-axe again. In an instant Milton regained his composure, pressing the gun into Angela's temple. She winced and squealed in pain. "Take another step and your friend dies."

Jacob froze about ten feet in front of Milton, whose eyes grew wide with fear. "She's here," he said. "I must go now."

"Who's here?" Kathleen said, knowing the answer. Liz was helping them. And Milton, or Maling, was very much afraid of her.

"You'll get instructions," he said, turning around, pushing Angela through the doorway, onto the veranda, and down the stairs. Then he dragged her roughly to the waiting truck, the gun still pinned to her head.

Jacob and Angela followed, stopping out on the porch, too afraid to move for fear Angela would get a bullet in the head for their efforts. They watched in dismay as Angela was kidnapped.

He stuffed her into the passenger seat, slammed the door and turned around, glaring at them. "Try and follow me and your friend dies. Call the cops and she dies."

"He won't kill her," Jacob said, as the truck peeled out of the driveway. "He wants the sword. Let's go after him."

"No, wait," Kathleen said, grabbing his arm. "Look at the violence he's capable of. Do you want to take a chance with Angela's life?"

Jacob jerked himself free from her grasp and started jumping around, flailing his arms spasmodically, the pick-axe gyrating closer to Kathleen. His eyes welled with tears. "What the fuck do we do? We can't do nothing, we can't call the cops, what the hell do you suggest?"

"Calm down, Jacob, please," Kathleen said, backing away. She was reluctant to go near him like this. "Let's get the sword, get out of here, and wait for his call. He needs that sword. He'll call us, don't worry."

Slowly his panicked movements stopped, his flailing arms returning to his sides, along with the pick-axe. Finally, he stood motionless, staring at Kathleen, seemingly waiting for instructions. His fearful expression suggested he was unable to think on his own.

Think. You're supposed to be the calm one. "Why don't you take a flashlight, go get a broom and some nails or something, clean up the mess and fix the door so we can close it properly. I'll go downstairs, get the sword and we'll go," she said.

He stared at her blankly for a few seconds. Finally he set the pick-axe down and went into the living room. He retrieved a flashlight and a walkie-talkie, returned outside and went over to an outbuilding.

"I'll be in the basement," she said. "I'll be up in a minute."

Entering the living room, Kathleen heard a meow. Spike entered from the kitchen, her glowing yellow eyes regarding her curiously. She had told Martha she would look after the cat, but doubted this one-time feral animal would travel without a fuss. She would probably have to feed and visit her regularly at Martha's house, and she didn't want to hang around here any longer than she had to.

"Spike. Come here, Spike. I won't hurt you."

The cat hissed, arched her back, and darted into the kitchen.

"You want some food," Kathleen said, following her. She noticed the food and water bowl were empty and started rummaging around the kitchen cabinets. She found a box of Meow Mix and poured some into a bowl. Spike approached her as she bent down, purring and rubbing up against her affectionately. She tried to pat her and the cat darted away, this time without hissing.

"It'll take time, but you'll like me," she said.

Spike meowed, staring at her curiously from a corner of the room.

She picked up the empty water bowl, rinsed it out, filled it with water and set it down beside the Meow Mix. Spike returned and crunched at the food, only glancing up at her this time as she slid the water bowl closer to the cat food. She purred softly while she ate.

"I was feeding Spike," she said, noticing Jacob screwing the deadbolt in as she returned to the living room. He had swept up the debris and also had a small piece of plywood leaning against the door, presumably to be inserted in the window casing as part of the repair.

He acknowledged her with a weak grin and continued working.

About twenty minutes later, Kathleen appeared in the living room holding the heavy, ornate gold sword. It glinted as she placed it on a coffee table. Jacob was just finishing the plywood installation as she sat down. He picked up his hammer and screwdriver, tossed them into a small metal toolbox, and stared at the sword.

"Nice, isn't it?" she said, gliding her hand lightly across the sharp blade and smiling. On initial contact, it had infused her with a rush of positive energy. She felt a vitality, a clarity of mind that she had never experienced in her lifetime before. She had thought of explaining the powerful force to Jacob, but thought better of it once she had sat down. Instead she said, "Feel it."

He sat down beside her and touched the blade. Immediately he beamed with happiness and the color returned to his pale features. "Wow. That's totally amazing!"

A few minutes later they rolled down the highway in Jacob's SUV, the sword glinting off the pale moonlight in the back seat. Kathleen's phone rang. It was a blocked number. She picked it up while Jacob listened.

"Hello."

"Do you have the sword?" It was the voice of Maling.

"Yes, we do. Is Angela safe?"

"Yes, she is."

"I want to talk to her," Jacob said.

"We want to talk to her," Kathleen said.

There was a moment's pause and Angela's panicked voice came on the line. Kathleen passed the phone to Jacob.

"Angela," he said. "Are you okay?"

"No," she said. "I'm scared. Get me out of here."

"Okay," Jacob said, but then Maling's voice came on the line and Jacob passed the phone to her. He had called Kathleen, after all.

"Tomorrow night at eleven," Maling said. "Poverty Beach. Bring the sword in exchange for the girl. Come alone."

"Jacob's coming with me," Kathleen said. "He's her boyfriend and if he doesn't come, he'll go to the police." She didn't know what else to say.

There was a long pause. "Okay, you and Jacob and that's all. I see another car, another person, she's dead. Tortured and killed. You got that?"

"Yeah," Kathleen said, and the line went dead.

CHAPTER TWENTY-THREE

Kathleen had been back to Martha's house earlier in the day to feed Spike. And, miraculously, she had been able to coax the cat into a small metal cat cage and bring her home. Spike sat on the couch, purring contentedly. It seemed to her Spike was just waiting for an opportunity to show them just how well-behaved she could be. Oh, sure she had meowed and cried during the twenty-two minute trip from Martha's acreage to Kathleen's apartment, but why wouldn't she?

It was the very first time she had ever travelled in a car.

After hiding under an armchair in Kathleen's apartment for three hours, Kathleen had finally coaxed Spike out with some treats and the cat had relaxed somewhat. She doubted Spike would ever relax completely, but she had lived most of her adult life having to fend for herself among other dangerous predators. If a car went by, someone in another unit flushed a toilet, or faint voices echoed from neighboring apartments, Spike raised an eye and would cautiously look around before settling back into her nap. She was a smart and edgy animal, but had certainly taken to Kathleen in a big way and in a very short time.

Although she sometimes hissed at Kathleen, Spike's bark was worse than her bite. Kathleen understood the hissing was a defense mechanism, developed from surviving in the wild. Spike had yet to bite or scratch her. Kathleen had even patted the cat a few times and come out of it unscathed.

Last night she had arrived home just before midnight. She had tried to sleep, but spent the night awake, tossing around and wondering if she should call Detective Redmond. She couldn't bring herself to pick up the phone, believing to do so would mean a gruesome end to Angela.

As she was about to set out this morning, Wednesday, March 14th, to complete a list of errands, Redmond had phoned, wanting to talk to her tonight. She had told him she wasn't feeling well and hoped as she had climbed into her Camry that the detective wouldn't spot her driving around.

Fortunately, she didn't notice Redmond as she bought a few groceries, some take-out food, and stopped briefly at the hospital to visit Mark and Martha before retrieving Spike.

Mark had been in a lot of pain when she saw him, but smiled at her and at the sight of the cheeseburger, fries, and Coke she had picked up from Wendy's on the way up.

Out of fear for her friend's life, she had not been able to bring herself to tell him about Angela's kidnapping. She had no idea how many followers Maling had recruited and how many of them might be lurking around the hallways of the hospital. She wasn't about to take any chances, at least not until Angela was safe. Besides, she had promised Jacob she would keep her mouth shut until after tonight.

Before leaving, she looked in on Martha, saw her sleeping fitfully, and left.

The woman's expression, even in sleep, had been contorted in pain and Kathleen hoped she would live. *But if she didn't, would she pass on to a better place?*

Kathleen hadn't given death a lot of thought up until the last week or so, when so much of it had decided to announce its fateful presence in this otherwise peaceful landscape. *But what of it? Is it so bad, would it be that bad, living in the spirit world?*

She didn't know. But she knew a lot of people didn't give it much thought; although it was one of the few certainties in life. *We live and we die. And, with any luck, as we're lying there in that death bed, or we see our life about to come to an end during an accident—a murder maybe—we can look back and not have any regrets about life. And, if we think we will have regrets, then now is the time to change.*

What is the future? An intangible we can never be certain about. What is the past? The past is history. What is the now? It's the only thing we have, so we need to make the best of it.

Spike meowed, snapping Kathleen away from her reflection. She stared at the cat curled comfortably a few feet away from her on the couch. "Hi, Spike," she said, after a pause. "Can I pat you?"

"Meow." Spike looked at her curiously.

Kathleen extended a hand and Spike hissed. She gently touched the cat's head. Spike purred.

She stared at the mysterious sword in front of her on the coffee table and slid her hand along its handle and along the blade. It still made her feel good, but the positive energy had lost some of its force. It entered her slowly, without the overwhelming, surging power she had felt earlier.

She stood up and walked into her kitchen. Spike bolted under the couch and hid. The cat wasn't, and probably never would be, used to sudden movements.

She swallowed two anti-anxiety pills with a glass of water and returned to the living room. In light of recent traumatic events, Dr. Heeling had increased her dosage again.

The phone rang as she entered the living room, Jacob's number appearing on the screen. She looked at the wall clock before picking it up: 9:57 pm. *Shit. It's almost time.*

"You ready?" he asked, after she said hello.

"Yeah."

"Okay, I'm on my way."

Kathleen pulled a large duffle bag from a hallway closet, placed a digital recorder, two flashlights, extra batteries, and a digital camera inside. She also slid the sword inside the bag, at least until they arrived at the beach.

A few minutes later they were inside the SUV, driving to Poverty Beach.

"Do we have a plan?" Jacob asked nervously.

"Well, I think we should both get out of the car, but leave the doors open, leave it running. Once he releases Angela I'll throw the sword out."

"I don't think we should try any funny stuff," he said. "I don't want to play hero when we're playing with Angela's life."

"Agreed," Kathleen said.

"You didn't tell anyone, did you?" he asked.

"No, I was up to see Mark today, didn't mention it to him."

"How is he? I meant to get up there."

"He's in a lot of pain right now, but he'll recover. He was pretty drugged up when I saw him."

Silence settled over them as Jacob drove along scenic Highway 17. Every once in a while they would get glimpses of the Atlantic Ocean, a black body of water flickering white as the moonlight and stars danced off its surface. It was a clear night, dead calm, the temperature agreeably mild.

A few minutes later, Jacob turned onto the narrow dirt road that would wind its way to the ocean before reaching it in a half mile or so. The small road was dark and the SUV bumped along as he decreased his speed to allow for the rugged terrain. They passed three or four houses on the way, but there weren't many. It was a secluded location even at the height of the tourist season in July.

Finally they pulled up alongside the water, halfway around the donut-shaped end of the road. There was no parking lot.

He put the vehicle in park, turned the lights off and they waited. There were a few small summer cottages dotting the road next to the SUV but the lights were off, nobody home.

Kathleen looked in the side view mirror as headlights suddenly approached behind them, rolling slowly along and parking about twenty feel behind the SUV. She shone the flashlight at the lights, could barely make out a red pick-up truck stopping.

"It's them," she said, removing the sword from the duffle bag.

"Let's get Angela and get out of here," Jacob said, stepping out of the vehicle.

Kathleen stepped out, leaving the door open, and the sword on the passenger seat.

Reverend James Maling in the body of Milton Blyster stepped out of the vehicle and closed the door.

Kathleen saw the pistol tucked in his pants and pointed the flashlight beam into the red pick-up. She saw Angela sitting in the passenger seat, her hands tied behind her back, her mouth gagged with a white cloth.

"The sword," Maling said.

"The girl," Jacob said.

What the hell are we doing in this remote beach at this time of night, unarmed? Kathleen thought. *We must be crazy.* "Let her out of the truck," she said. "We want to make sure she's okay. Then I'll get you the sword."

Maling pulled the passenger door open, gun drawn. "Get out. And stay here, until I say."

Angela stumbled her way out of the truck.

Maling slammed the door. "The sword."

Kathleen lifted it off the passenger seat and flung it into the air. It landed blade first, sticking into the sand at a perfect ninety-degree angle.

Maling stared at it, recoiling.

"Oh no," he said. "Pick it up. Put it in the back of the truck." He was afraid to touch it.

Jacob took one step and Maling trained the gun on him. "Not you, her!"

Kathleen took a few steps, picked up the sword, approached the truck being careful to give Maling a wide berth, and flung it into the truck bed. It clanged loudly, the sound echoing eerily though the night for a second or two before dying out.

Angela was already running when Maling fired the first shot, puncturing the SUV's rear tire, the air escaping with a whooshing sound. Kathleen heard the crack of the gun and dove at him. He sidestepped and she crashed head-first into the red truck and stumbled to the ground, dazed.

She got up, staggered into a thicket of bushes and dove to the ground, feeding on the adrenaline of self-preservation.

He ran around to the driver door and fired two more shots, one of them penetrating the back of Angela's head just as Jacob tackled her into a row of small bushes. She screamed, slumping forward in his arms as Maling blindly fired two more times into the dark brush before closing the door and backing up along the narrow road.

Kathleen saw him disappear around the corner. She could still see headlights fading, and hear Jacob's horrified voice yelling, "Call 911 ... call 911 ... for fuck sakes, somebody call 911," when something unexpected happened.

The red pick-up truck stopped, not two hundred feet away. She could see the lights, hear the engine revving. *Oh shit, he's coming back. He's coming back to kill us.* And then she noticed it. Another vehicle's lights were coming down the road, heading toward Maling.

Jacob was still yelling and screaming as she pulled out her cell phone and speed-dialed Detective Redmond.

"Angela's been shot in the head," Jacob said, his voice rising.

"I'm calling," she said.

Redmond picked up on the first ring. "Angela's been shot in the head," she said. "We're at Poverty Beach."

"Shit," Redmond said angrily. "When are you kids going to let me in on things?" And, before she could answer, "Is that you in the vehicle, leaving the beach?"

"No," Kathleen said, suddenly realizing the detective was driving right for a possessed madman. "It's Maling, and he's got a gun."

The phone went dead and she stared wide-eyed and horrified at the trail of white lights on a dark night. Maling had begun accelerating, going straight for Redmond. Suddenly she heard gunshots, then a windshield shattering. One vehicle skidded into the ditch, the other drove on toward the highway. In the darkness, she could not interpret what had happened.

By this time, Jacob leaned against the side of his vehicle, cradling Angela's bleeding head and sobbing. As the sound of the approaching vehicle drew nearer, Kathleen ran to Jacob, lifted the limp body of Angela and carried her into the bushes. Jacob followed, still cradling Angela's blood-soaked head in his arms. They crouched down and waited. The lights grew brighter.

"Shut up," she said to Jacob. "He might be coming back." They panted in the bushes, watching the headlights grow, two luminescent eyes coming right at them.

The vehicle stopped. A door opened.

"Kathleen," Detective Redmond said. "Where the hell are you?"

CHAPTER TWENTY-FOUR

Kathleen and Jacob sat and drank coffee in the King's County Memorial Hospital waiting room at 3:00 in the morning on Thursday, March 15th. Redmond had reacted swiftly, determining that Angela had a pulse and rushing her to the hospital, along with Kathleen and Jacob.

The detective had taken a bullet as Maling had floored the small pick-up at him and began wildly shooting out the open side window. After one bullet had shattered the windshield, the other tearing through his left shoulder, Redmond had thought it wise to yield the right of way.

He had skidded to a stop into the shallow ditch, navigating his car with his good arm, before rescuing them. If it hadn't been for Kathleen's last-minute call, he would have been able to pursue the escaping vehicle. As it was, he had to rescue Angela, so Maling had slipped away into the night.

On the way to the hospital, Redmond had been livid with Kathleen for withholding information. He had calmed a little when she explained that Maling had threatened to kill Angela if they told anyone.

The detective grunted and winced as she outlined the story, but seemed to take it all in with a degree of sincerity. In view of what had been happening around town lately, he wasn't prepared to rule out anything anymore.

"I hope we hear something soon," Jacob said, rising and walking over to the vending machine. Angela and Redmond were both being operated on. "Want another coffee?" he asked, plugging some change into the machine.

"No, thanks. Still got some. Can we get your vehicle tomorrow ... I mean later today, in the afternoon?"

"No problem," he said, pulling out a paper cup that had partially filled with hot coffee, milk and sugar. "How come these things never fill up to the top?" He showed her the contents of the cup. "Look, it's barely half full."

The door to the waiting room opened and a young male surgeon walked in, his green surgical scrubs splattered red on the chest. He still had the signature green cap wrapped snuggly around his head, the white partial face mask dangling around his neck. "You're Angela's friends?" he asked, as Jacob sat beside Kathleen.

Jacob inhaled deeply as Kathleen studied the man's green eyes, searching for a sign of trouble.

"Yeah," they said in unison. They couldn't have timed their responses better if they had wanted to.

"I'm Peter Dunlevy. Your friend is lucky to be alive."

They both sighed.

"The bullet didn't actually penetrate her skull. It connected at an odd angle, shattered a few pieces of her skull into the back of her brain and landed somewhere else."

"Is she going to be okay?" Jacob asked.

"There might be some brain damage, but the prognosis looks good. From what we could tell, the bits of her skull only very slightly damaged the back of her brain. We just have to wait and see."

"How's she doing now?" Jacob asked.

"She's under anesthetic still. You two should go home, get some sleep."

The doctor turned to walk away.

"What about Detective Redmond?" Kathleen asked.

He stopped and turned to face her. "Oh, he's okay. We've removed the bullet, and he's resting. But it's too late to visit him, if that's what you're wondering."

"That's fine, thanks," Kathleen said, and he left.

She was physically and mentally drained and wanted to be home in bed.

A few minutes later, as they waited for a taxi in the main lobby of the hospital, Kathleen couldn't help but wonder what terrible fate might await them now that the ancient sword, their only hope for survival, had disappeared. *God only knows.*

CHAPTER TWENTY-FIVE

Kathleen had finally drifted off, after tossing for about an hour after arriving home. She had nightmares of horrific images of death and bloodshed, mixed with images of God and redemption. In one nightmare she watched horrified as Maling walked down Main Street Montague, stabbing pedestrians with the ancient sword. Blood sprayed. People screamed. People died. It seemed he had transformed the positive force of the weapon into one of murderous, evil carnage.

Suddenly, Maling spotted her. "You. You die."

He began chase.

In the dark of the night, Kathleen ran. She rounded a corner and Liz appeared, a large white apparition floating down from the heavens. Liz took her arm. "Follow me."

Liz guided her into a safe house and disappeared. Panicking, Kathleen wandered around aimlessly in complete blackness. Suddenly she felt the walls closing in on her. Trapped in a small dark room, she didn't know where she was, how to escape. Then, clunking footsteps growing louder. She knew with an eerie certainty the footsteps were Maling's and he was coming to kill her, put her out of her misery, her panic attacks, her life of nervousness and worry.

As the deafeningly loud footsteps neared, she had bolted upright in her bed terrified and sweat-drenched. After staring out the window at the rays of moonlight shining through her Venetian blinds, she had become inspired to write a poem.

In her college days, she had written many poems and found the exercise of creating very liberating and therapeutic.

If I can get it down, maybe I can go back to sleep peacefully, she had thought, noticing it was 6:30 in the morning.

So she had walked into her office, sat at her laptop and typed:

Disarrayed thoughts:

What if they don't know I'm gone?
How will they know where to look?
Would they ever suppose I'm stuck down here in this nook?

Would someone just help me find my way?
Just go wherever, is what they say.
It really doesn't matter which way I go,
I need some help, please you must know.

Why is nothing ever as it seems?
It's hard to learn when it's all a dream.
If something made sense for a change,
It all would be really strange.

For you see the words get mixed up in my head.
I wish they'd all be pictures instead.
Because I'm not myself you see;
And that's why I'm in this sleepy hollow tree.

I'm late for what? I can't recall.
Tick-tock repeats the clock on the wall.

"Don't paint the roses red," she said.
"Don't lose your temper, or it's off with your head."

The doorknob opens with a small key.
Do you even remember me?
I fell asleep; I had a dream.
What is this world? Where have I been?

I can't explain myself you see,
That must mean I need more tea.
The dream is over, it's now dead.
But I am still inside my head.

No time for tears, no time for fears.
The time has come to go my dear.
You must go back to get to the end.
You must fall forward once again.

And when you see the world that was,
Remember why they're there because,
A world without them would not be,
A finer place for you and me.

Reading it now, after sleeping most of the day away, comforted her, liberated her from the frightening thoughts that had flooded her mind during and after the nightmare. She wasn't even sure of the poem's meaning, but knew if she came back to it in the future, it would become clear. That's the way it went with her poems.

Unless I'm in you and you're in me. Maybe that's the last line. Don't be silly. That doesn't make any sense. Or does it?

She stared at the two pills on the coffee table before finally tossing them into her mouth and washing them down with a glass of water. She would be good for a little longer. For how much longer, she didn't know.

Spike, dozing on the couch, raised an eye at her curiously. She noticed the time was 8:36 pm (*where had the day gone?*) and decided to call Jacob. He should be back from visiting Angela and Mark. Kathleen had thought about making the trip earlier, but had changed her mind, deciding instead to take some much needed alone time. *Or by myself,* she thought. She didn't like the word alone as it suggested lonely and Kathleen was seldom lonely. She liked her own company and now the company of Spike.

Jacob also planned on coming over tonight. They were going to attempt to contact Liz again.

She got him on the phone and he gave her a brief summary of his day. He had decided not to bother her about his vehicle and had retrieved it with the help of a friend. He had gone to the hospital. Mark was doing well. "He said hi and he loves you." Angela was groggy but actually talking, which he viewed as nothing short of a miracle. She seemed a little dopey, but otherwise cognitive.

Martha Pelletier had gone into shock, the result of the burns, and died last night.

And Detective Redmond had undergone a successful surgery and discharged himself from the hospital.

A lump formed in Kathleen's throat as she digested the news about Martha. *Everyone's dying. I've got to stop this!*

"Are you coming over?" she asked.

"I'm on my way. Oh, one more thing," he said.

"What?" Kathleen asked, expecting more bad news.

"Detective Redmond called me today."

"What did he want?"

"He made me promise to call him if we have any leads."

"Okay," Kathleen said, remembering she had screened one of his earlier calls. She sent him a quick text message, informing him he would be the first to know, should any new leads arrive.

A little while later, Kathleen sat on the couch, Jacob on the armchair and Spike under the couch. They had been there fifteen minutes and Kathleen had been calling out to Liz with no success. They waited for a response.

"I don't think this is going to work," Jacob said. "Ghosts don't come out on demand."

"We've been doing this a long time. We've heard noises, doors closing and other stuff on demand."

"That's true. Keep going then."

"It's not like we have a lot of choices, is it?" It was a rhetorical question.

Kathleen tried a different tact. "Elizabeth Pelletier, your family name is getting extinguished by Reverend Maling and we must do something. Martha Pelletier just died from her burns. Do you want more people to die? Please help us."

They waited a minute or so in silence.

Suddenly the lamp flickered, the room became cold.

Spike hissed, meowed loudly and darted down the hall and into Kathleen's bedroom.

Abruptly, Kathleen's facial features contorted angrily, her eyes glazing over with a faraway stare. In a voice that sounded nothing like her own, she said, "I'm in you and you're in me."

"What?" Jacob asked, unable to recognize Kathleen's voice.

He felt his heart rate increase, breathed deeply a few times. He wanted to take a chapter out of Spike's book and run away. *It's now or never, buddy. Calm yourself the fuck down and get the information.*

An audio-video camera, a separate digital recorder, documented the events.

"Are you Elizabeth Pelletier?" he asked.

The faraway look slowly focused on him, the eyes opening with surprise as Liz registered him, the house, her new body. "Yes," she said in a shrill voice.

This is spirit attachment. Channeling. "Can you lead us to Maling, to the ancient sword?"

Liz's expression became grim. "Reverend James Maling raped and murdered me. Nobody knows. I was discredited, but he's the evil one."

"That's what we're trying to prevent," he said. "More of his evil. We have to find him, find the sword. Can you please lead us to him? Please, please ... people are dying!"

"Follow me," she said, standing. "Evil is close."

It was all he could do to grab a flashlight and a jacket to keep up with her as she left. He walked down the stairs behind her, speed-dialing Detective Redmond.

"I need you to come to Kathleen's street right away," he said when the detective answered. "You'll see me. I'm walking down the street with ... uh ... Kathleen."

"I'll be right over," the detective said, and hung up.

A few minutes later, Detective Redmond stood on the porch of an old brick two-story home on a quiet residential street, about a block and a half from Kathleen's house. Liz stood behind him, staring zombie-like. Jacob was behind her. He stepped onto the porch, searching her face.

"Where's Maling? Where's the sword?" he asked.

"Maling's upstairs in the bedroom. The sword is in a treasure chest in the basement."

"I'm going in," Redmond said.

"Aren't you going to call for back-up?" Jacob asked. "You're not in very good shape."

"Yeah, right," he said with a curious expression. "What am I going to say? We have a possessed woman leading us to a possessed man hiding a sword that can save the human race? How do you think that'll go over with the boys?"

As an afterthought, Redmond pulled out a small pistol from a leather holster on his ankle and handed it to Jacob. "This is a complete breach of police protocol, but are you up for this?"

"Sure," Jacob said, pointing to the body of Kathleen. "But what about her?"

She answered the question for them. She shoved Redmond aside, kicked open the door and stepped inside the house.

They followed.

Redmond noticed it first, then Jacob. The smell of death permeated the old home. A decapitated elderly man sat on the living room couch, his head on his lap, drenched in blood. An old woman, or what remained of her, reclined in a Lazy Boy chair. Her body and face had multiple stab wounds and her intestines were strewn around her lap.

A small boy, perhaps ten-years-old, lay face-up on the floor, three gunshot wounds to his head and a deep X-mark slashed across his chest, his mouth twisted in fear. A pool of blood surrounded him.

They had been dead for some time and the smell was sickening. Jacob felt the vomit rise up in his throat and fought to contain it, coughing and putting a hand to his face with a grimace.

Redmond winced at the sight and smell of the macabre murder scene.

Liz seemed not to notice. "Come out and face your demons," she said, methodically walking down the hall.

"Go into the basement, get the sword," Redmond instructed. "I'll get Maling."

Jacob disappeared into the basement, shining his flashlight down the rickety stairs. He heard shots being fired upstairs as he picked up a nearby sledge hammer and gave the only treasure chest he could find a good wack, breaking the steel lock on the first swing.

There it was. The sword.

Lucky, lucky, now get upstairs with that thing.

He grabbed the sword, ran up the stairs, two at a time, feeling energized by its powerful force.

Maling (in the body of Milton Blyster) and Redmond exchanged gunfire in the stairwell, Redmond on the main floor, Maling upstairs.

"I told you to throw your weapon down and get on the floor with your hands outstretched," Redmond shouted.

Liz sat at the kitchen table, the same glazed look, humming a tune, unintelligible to Jacob. She stopped humming, staring at the sword as he approached.

"Stay out of the way," Redmond said to Jacob as Maling answered the detective's directive with a bullet that whistled past them, smashing into the plaster wall.

"You can't conquer evil," Maling said. "Go home." He appeared at the landing and fired another shot, but Redmond and Jacob anticipated it and dove into the hallway. Jacob lost his grip on the sword and it clanged along the floor, skidding into the wall and sticking into the tall baseboard.

Liz rose from her chair, grabbed the sword and stepped over Redmond and Jacob, before they could pick themselves up.

"No," Jacob yelled. "Stay here." But it was too late. She brandished the sword in front of her with a fiery grin and walked up the stairs toward Maling.

He fired one, two, three shots but they missed, the last one ricocheting off the blade and digging into the ceiling. Redmond scrambled up behind Liz, firing. One bullet sliced into Maling's shoulder and he fell back with a thud.

Liz reached the landing. She now had the sword extended toward the fallen Maling. She brought it down slowly to his chest as he grabbed his gun, pointed it at her head and pulled the trigger.

With maybe a hundredth of a second to spare, Redmond shoved her out of the way, shot Maling in the heart, took the bullet meant for Liz in his other shoulder, and slumped on Maling, knocking his gun across the floor and into an adjacent bedroom.

Jacob grabbed the sword next to Kathleen, who lay on the hallway floor stunned, blinking her eyes, trying to make sense of the situation. Jacob rolled Redmond away and pressed the blade to the dying man's chest. They didn't know it at the time, but they would never be able to discuss what happened next.

Jacob's hands trembled as the sword vibrated. He felt an indescribable, all-consuming, black, evil force flow up the blade, stop at the handle, permeate the entire second floor with an enveloping dark mist and then evaporate and disappear a split second later, an eerie hissing sound trailing its exit.

He was not able to put into words the dark thoughts that had invaded his mind during that brief period.

But when the mist cleared they were all smiling.

"What just happened?" Kathleen asked, wiping her eyes. "Where am I?" The last thing she could remember was sitting on her couch, calling for Liz to appear.

Redmond grunted, a small pool of blood forming around his other injured shoulder. He couldn't move either arm. His ribs ached. "Someone call 911."

CHAPTER TWENTY-SIX

Sunday, March 25th, 1:15 pm, Brudenell Point Cemetery, Prince Edward Island.

It was a mass funeral. There were services going on all around them and Kathleen heard faint echoes of other eulogies as the priest stood over the sunken casket of Nick Calibri and talked.

"For those who knew Nick well, they would say he was a fine, God-fearing man who cared deeply for his friends and family. They would say he would help his fellow man, loan him money, give him the shirt off his back. They would also say he had a soft spot for his son Henry and would do anything for the young boy. Nick should have lived a long, productive, happy life but let us be clear here ..." The bald priest coughed and cleared his throat.

"What happened to this young man was not a manifestation of God. Oh no, this was not God's doing. What happened on that fateful day in the Holy Trinity Church was the work of the Devil. The evil power of the Devil had a grip on this young man, on many people of Montague and our neighbor, Georgetown. We not only mourn the loss of Nick Calibri, we mourn the loss of many fine members of our community. And I am here today not only to bestow Nick's spirit into the kingdom of God, but to tell you how you can prevent yourself from this evil possession. During the hunt for the demon, someone discovered an ancient sword that rids people of evil spirits. Oh, I know what you're saying. You're saying I must be crazy. But no, I'm afraid you'll have to think again."

The priest studied the mourners and then continued: "We have this sword displayed at the King's Playhouse Theatre. All you have to do is go there and touch it and then tell me I'm crazy. I personally know dozens of residents who have touched it and been cured of the evil powers that had possessed them. Go there, touch it."

He opened his arms and looked up to the bright blue sky. "But that's only part of the reason we are gathered here today. We are here to safely see the passage of Nick's soul into the kingdom of heaven. I hereby commit your soul to the Father, the Son and the Holy Spirit. May you have everlasting peace and happiness in your new life in heaven. Amen."

"Amen," some of the funeral-goers said. The priest lifted a handful of dirt, threw it down on the casket, picked up his Bible and began consoling some immediate family members who had begun sobbing.

Kathleen picked up a handful of dirt, dropped it on the sunken casket and wiped a tear from her eye. She was followed by a procession of family and friends, including Angela, Jacob and Mark.

Mark had been released from hospital and his burns were healing well.

Jacob was seeing much less of the black cloud lately and a lot more of Angela. He had visited her daily in the hospital. She had been released this morning and was living with him at his apartment until her house sold and they would be able to buy a home together. They had become an item. She drew the odd blank when she spoke, but was otherwise the same Angela they knew and loved. Only time would tell how much brain damage she had actually suffered.

The two couples walked arm-in-arm across the lawn to Black Death, who had been cleared of any wrongdoing, repaired and released on his own recognizance. It was a bright and sunny day, the tell-tale sights and sounds of spring in the air.

Since Martha's death, Kathleen had inherited Spike, whom she had grown to adore.

They had never solved the identity of the entity that had wreaked havoc at Angela's house but knew some aspects of the paranormal couldn't be solved.

After Kathleen's visit to the anxiety treatment center, her medication had been changed to Thorazine. She found herself much less troubled, more energetic and often able to get a good night's sleep. She knew she still had a lot of grieving ahead of her, but she felt much better prepared to deal with it than before.

She had even confided in the vice-principal about her condition and he had been sympathetic. And, after Linda Wellington left the autism class for another job, teacher Ron Baglund had learned a few things about control. Apparently, he had learned to control everybody would mean the loss of his best people. He had even confided in Kathleen he liked her work and hoped she would stay.

Kathleen had also followed up on a number of the paranormal contact requests and many of the respondents claimed the spirits were no longer haunting them. She had whittled down a list of 76 inquiries to 26, and the inquiries were no longer coming in fast and furious.

As they climbed into Black Death, Detective Blaine Redmond rolled up in a black unmarked police car, a uniformed officer driving. He pressed a button and the window rolled down. Both of his arms were in slings. "How you guy's doing?"

"Good," Kathleen said, as her friends waved.

"Seems like the sword's working," he said. "I see a lot less freaks walking around town."

She nodded.

"Hey, I wanted to ask you something."

"Oh, what's that?" Kathleen asked.

"Are you still planning on carrying on with the ghost hunting?"

She looked at her friends. They nodded.

"It looks that way," she said. "Why?"

"I just wanted to say that if you have any more trouble with ghosts, don't call me." He paused for effect. "I'll call you."

They laughed as Redmond grinned and the vehicle drove away.

"Why don't we go to Pizza Delight?" Angela asked, as they rolled into town a few minutes later. "I'm hungry."

"Me too," Jacob said, kissing her on the cheek. He sat with his arm around her in the back seat.

"Sounds good," Mark said, lifting a hand from the steering wheel, leaning over and pecking Kathleen on the cheek. "See, two can play at that game."

"I'm in," Kathleen said. "I could use a drink anyway."

A minute later Mark looked over at Kathleen curiously. "Hey, you know we haven't talked about something for a long time?"

"What's that?" Kathleen asked.

"The house. I want to buy a house for us to live in. What do you think?"

Kathleen grinned. "I have one problem with that."

"What's that?"

"I have another friend."

"A what?"

"Another friend, Spike. She's our new black cat baby."

He laughed. "Spike's welcome."

"Good, I'd love to move in with you."

A few minutes later they were quiet as Mark pulled Black Death into the Pizza Delight parking lot.

I'm in you and you're in me.

"What did you say?" Kathleen asked Mark, who only stared at her, shaking his head blankly.

She turned to Jacob and Angela. "You guys say something?"

"No," Jacob said, while Angela shook her head.

"Why, did you hear something?" Mark asked.

"No, I guess not."

Also by William Blackwell

Phantom Rage, Poison Rage, Infected Rage
Nightmare's Edge
Resurrection Point
Brainstorm
A Head for an Eye
Rule 14
Blood Curse
Black Dawn
Assaulted Souls
Assaulted Souls II
Assaulted Souls III
The Strap
The End is Nigh
Orgon Conclusion
Freaky Franky
The Witch's Tombstone
The Dark Menace
In Your Dreams
Macabre Alley
Tales of Damnation

Poison Rage, The Rage Trilogy: Book # 2 Preview

"*Poison Rage* is an excellent second installment to The Rage Trilogy. Blackwell's talent is obvious as he slowly builds tension right to the very end. It kept me on the edge of my seat wondering what would happen next." -Amazon

"A riveting read." -Amazon

"*Poison Rage* slowly but surely manipulates your mind and you'll find yourself in the middle of a twisted story, frightened to your teeth, and hardly able to even breathe." -Goodreads

As a strung-out team of paranormal investigators approach the shocking truth surrounding deadly rage-filled attacks in an unassuming small town, dangerous roadblocks quickly emerge.

Kathleen Freeborne discovers their inner demons are preventing them from getting to the bottom of the sudden and violent outbursts. Her once loyal and loving boyfriend has suddenly become distant and cold, withdrawing into an alcoholic abyss. Her best friend starts keeping disturbing secrets from the team and retreating into a catatonic shell of her former self.

Meanwhile, Detective Blaine Redmond, close to learning the disturbing truth behind the uncontrolled aggression possessing unsuspecting townsfolk, abruptly vanishes.

Including extensive research from actual paranormal investigations, Poison Rage is a chilling and mind-bending examination of haunted happenings that paranormal investigators—often in the face of life-threatening consequences—choose to confront.

About the Author

Canadian dark fiction author William Blackwell studied journalism at Mount Royal University and English literature at The University of British Columbia. He worked as a journalist and a newspaper editor for many years before pursuing his passion for storytelling. His novels have been characterized as graphic, edgy, and at times terrifying. Currently living on a secluded acreage on Prince Edward Island, Blackwell finds much of his inspiration from Mother Nature, odd people, traveling, and bizarre nightmares.

Author Comments

Thank you for reading this book. I would be eternally grateful if you would post a book review on your favorite book retailer website. A positive review is the highest compliment a writer can receive. Reviews are crucial to the success of any author and they help readers discover new books. You don't have to say much. A few sentences will suffice.

In other news, I have a gift for you. Complete the signup form below with your name and email address and download a FREE copy of *Resurrection Point*, a dark tale about the horrifying consequences of experimenting with death and resurrection. You're only agreeing to be kept up to date on blog posts, new releases, and freebies. I promise I won't spam you and you can unsubscribe at any time.

Thanks again for your support.

http://www.wblackwell.com/free-ebook/

www.ingramcontent.com/pod-product-compliance
Lightning Source LLC
Chambersburg PA
CBHW020638180626
46816CB00003B/1024